Connect with Denora

Facebook: https://www.facebook.com/AuthorDenora

Instagram: @mzboone81

Twitter: @mzboone27

Note: This is a work of fiction. Names, characters, places and incidents either are products of the author's imagination or are used fictitiously. Any resemblance to actual events or locales or persons, living or dead, is entirely coincidental

Anointed Inspirations Publishing is currently accepting Christian Fiction submissions. For consideration please send completed manuscripts to

Anointedinspirationspublishing@gmail.com

Just A little while ago…

Kammy

It was the last day of school and I was so excited. As soon as school was over we were going to Disney World. I was happy that my friend Chelsea and JJ were going with us. We were going to have so much fun.

Jessica and Tamela were mad when I told them that I was going because they couldn't go. They always picked at me when they did something that I couldn't do. I bet they would want to be my friends when we got back to school.

The bell hadn't rang yet but the front office just called to let me know my Daddy was here. I was so happy that I didn't have to wait until the end of school to leave. Everybody else had a few more hours of school but not me.

I got my stuff and said by to my class, all except Jessica and Tamela, and ran to the car. I hopped in and buckled my seat belt.

"Hi Daddy!" I said smiling.

"You ready to go see Elsa and Oloft?" he asked me.

"Yep! I can't wait. I'm going to tell Elsa all about my room and maybe she will come visit one day." I told him.

"That would be nice baby. Here call mommy and let her know that I have you." He said handing me his phone.

“Yes hello?” Mommy said answering her phone.

“Hi Mommy!”

“Kammy?” she asked sounding like she didn’t know my voice.

“Yes it’s me. Daddy picked me up early.” I told her.

“Kammy. Bryce is still here he hasn’t left to come get you yet.” She said. Mommy didn’t sound right.

“Not Daddy Bryce Mommy. Daddy Drew.” I told her.

“OH MY GOD NOOOOOOOOOOOOOO! BRYCEEEEEEEEE!” she screamed as Daddy took the phone from me.

“Checkmate.” Was all he said to her and I knew something was wrong. I don’t think I’m going to Disney World.

Bryce

As I sat there looking at the small pink casket with the big blown up picture of Kammy beside it, all I felt was pure rage. I had just gotten the chance to love and raise the daughter that I created with the love of my life openly and here I am mourning her death at the hands of the person that was supposed to protect her. She had only been here for six years and just like that she was taken away from us. Kammy should have been enjoying a carefree childhood with parents, a sister, and friends loving her unconditionally but instead my precious baby girl was no longer here.

I looked over to Jewel whose face held no emotions. Not even one tear fell from her eyes and to everyone on the outside it may have looked like she didn't care. That assumption couldn't have been further from the truth. She had just gotten to the point where so many tears had been shed I honestly believe that her body was void of any more. I had been so worried the day that everyone found out about Drew's indiscretions. The last thing we wanted was for her to slip back into a deep depression. Although she hadn't then, this situation with Kammy had sent her over the edge. It had gotten so bad that we had to admit her to the psych ward at Carolina's Medical Center. She wouldn't eat, her sleep pattern was off and all she did was rock and moan. I hated to see her in this state and I would do my best to help her through this. That is when she decided to let me back in.

Jewel was feeling a pain that no mother should have to ever experience. Because she didn't know how to deal with it all she just shut everyone out, including me and Avery. After a week of searching for Kammy non-stop we had finally gotten a call that we prayed would bring us good news. Instead Detective Morrison called to let us know that they had found a body behind an abandoned house on Tuckaseegee Road and it was burned beyond recognition. The only way they were able to identify it was because of a charm bracelet that was on the child's right arm. Most of it had melted from the heat but it just so happened that one of the charms of a bunny was still intact. Kammy loved rabbits and her mother had gotten her that charm for her sixth birthday earlier in the year so we knew that it was her. From that day on Jewel hadn't said a word to anyone. It wasn't until I found her sprawled out on her bathroom floor with pills all around her that I knew I had to get her some help. Jewel had hit a deadly low and if she hadn't gotten some help in time she would have been dead too.

Avery sat on the opposite side of me as I put my arm around her shoulders and pulled her closer to me. I could feel the warm tears hitting my dress shirt as she silently cried. If there was ever a bond between sisters that was so tight it was between those two. Kammy adored her big sister and the feeling was definitely mutual. When Avery wasn't hanging with her friends she made sure to spend as much time as she could with her. Especially since she was about to go off to college.

My focus returned back to the front just as the pastor ended his eulogy. He said the final prayer as everyone stood up and the pallbearers took their places beside the casket. This was about to be the final goodbye once we arrived at the cemetery and as bad as it hurt we had to say goodbye. Just as I put my hand on the metal bar to lift the casket from its stand Jewel jumped up.

"THIS IS ALL YOUR FAULT!" she yelled looking right at me. I was taken aback because I had no idea what she was talking about.

"Baby what's wrong?" I asked her in a calming voice. She may have been hurt but that wasn't a reason to go off on me.

"You know what I'm talking about! You did this. You are the one that was out to get me from the start." Now she was in my face pointing her finger at me with her emotions flowing down her face.

"Jewel just calm down." I said reaching out to her as she slapped me across my face.

"Calm down? Calm down! Why did you do this to me Drew? I gave you everything. My heart, my soul, my body." She cried.

It was then that I understood that with everything that has happened to her she had checked out completely and I didn't know if she would come back from it this time. All because of a man. A man that was supposed to love and protect his family but had caused more heartache than one could imagine. The police had no leads on where Drew was but I knew that in due time his hiding place would be revealed. And when it was it would take the strength of all of God's angels to stop me from doing what I had planned for him.

Jewel kicked and screamed and cried so much that the orderlies that had accompanied her to the funeral had to restrain her and lead her out of the church. Not only did my heart ache because my daughter was dead but for Jewel as well. Watching the woman I loved go through what she was going through tore me to pieces and I didn't know how to comfort her but I would do my best.

My father along with Jewel's father, her brother Chris, Avery's boyfriend James, and James' father Jerrod we picked up my baby girl and headed towards the back of the church. Just as we were about to head out two uniformed police officers walked in with the Detective that had been in charge of Kammy's case leading the way.

"Please tell me that you have found Drew." I said as I held my breath.

"No we haven't found Drew but we were able to get a warrant for a suspect in her murder." Detective Morrison said.

"Praise God!" said Jewel's mother.

"Do you have him in custody?" I asked.

"Not yet." He stated simply.

"What do you mean not yet?" I asked. I didn't understand what he was telling me. If they had a suspect and a warrant for their arrest why were they here instead of arresting the monster that caused my family so much pain?

Before I could ask any other questions my father stepped in.

"If you have the person responsible and it's not Drew then who in the world could it be?" he questioned.

The look in the detective's eyes let me know that something was terribly wrong but none of us knew what it was.

"Why are you here when you should be out arresting the person that killed my sister?" Avery wanted to know.

"That's what we are here for." The one officer said as he took out his handcuffs.

I looked around the church trying to figure out who it could be because before they got taken away I was definitely going to get a piece of them. There was a tightening in my chest as the officer continued talking.

"Bryce Crenshaw you are under arrest for the murder of Kameron Milan Webber. You have the right to remain silent. Anything you say can and will be used against you in the court of law." The officer said as my world came to an end while being led out of the church.

Avery

This had to be the longest two weeks of my life. Instead of getting ready to enjoy my last summer at home before I headed off to college I was burying my little sister. Dealing with this kind of pain was something no one should ever have to deal with especially a parent. Children were supposed to bury their parents only once they have lived a fulfilling life, not the other way around. As much as I hurt for my sister I knew that the pain my mother and father were feeling was so much worse.

It still baffled me that the man I had called my father all of these years had been the one to cause all of this. I knew Bryce wasn't the one to kill Kammy. Although we had just recently learned he was our real father his love for us had gained strength like no other. This had Drew written all over it and I couldn't wait for God to reveal it. He better pray that the police found him before Daddy did because the look on his face as he was being led out of the church let me know that when he did see Drew it wasn't about to be anything nice.

Thinking back to the day of the kidnapping I recalled this feeling of grief washing over me and I didn't understand why. I remember I was in my room talking and laughing with my now fiancé James on the phone as I started to organize the things I would be taking with me when it was finally time to go as well as packing for our Disney trip. I still couldn't believe that we were engaged and even though we were excited about our future together we wanted to wait a while before saying those vows. I wanted my first marriage to be my last and I knew it would take time to make sure this was what we both wanted. Sadly to say I didn't want to end up in a marriage like my mother had so James and I both decided to learn from her mistakes and take our time.

"Did you see the look on Mr. Bryce's face when I pulled out that ring?" James asked before laughing at the memory.

"Did I? I thought for sure he was about to come across that table right along with your dad." I laughed.

"I'm just glad that our mothers were there to help us out."

“So am I. What time are you guys leaving for the airport?” I wanted to know. I couldn’t wait for our family trip and Kammy had been wanting to go to Disney World for the longest. I was actually excited too. I may have been almost grown but I don’t care what anyone said, Mickey Mouse would bring the kid out of anyone.

Before James had a chance to respond I heard my mother screaming Kammy’s name.

“I gotta go! I’ll call you right back.” I said rushing off of the phone and not giving him a chance to even reply.

I don’t know how I took two stairs at a time going down without falling flat on my face but I guess the adrenalin caused me no to pay attention to that at the moment. I needed to get to my mother and find out what was going on. There was so much fear in her voice that I was crying before I even made my way into the living room.

Entering the room at the same time with daddy he made it just in time to catch her before she hit the floor alongside the phone she had dropped. I don't remember a time where I have ever seen my mother this distraught about anything. Not even when she found out her husband was cheating on and using her all of these years was she this upset.

"Drew took my baby Bryce. He got my baby!" she wailed.

"Wait what? Calm down and try and tell me what happened." Bryce said trying to get an understanding of what she was talking about.

It took a few minutes but she was finally able to get out as much as she could.

“My phone rang with an unknown number. Usually I don’t answer those but something told me to. When I answered it was Kammy. She told me that her daddy had picked her up early. I didn’t understand what she mean because I knew that you were still here and hadn’t left yet. I told her that and she was like she meant that her daddy Drew had picked her up.

Before she could say anything else he took the phone and all he said was ‘checkmate’”. She explained before she broke down all over again.

Without either of them telling me what to do next I rushed over to get the phone from its position on the floor. Dialing 911 I waited for an operator before telling her what had happened. Not even ten minutes later the police were knocking at our door ready to get all of the information they could in order to start the search for my sister.

It was crucial that we found her within the first twenty four hours because they said after that her chances of survival would slowly begin to disintegrate. None of us wanted to hear that but the detectives wanted us to know just how important it was for them to have all of the information that they could in order to get the ball rolling.

After what felt like hours, they finally stopped questioning us long enough to set up wire taps on all of our phones. When mommy told them that Drew had a plan to take all of her money and how the women came into play they figured that he took Kammy in order to get a ransom for her. I knew that whatever he wanted she would pay just to get her back and if that meant her going broke do it she would. I just prayed that it all worked out in our favor before it was too late.

Constance

I sat inside of our hotel room in Rock Hill, South Carolina which was about fifteen minutes outside of Charlotte. As soon as everything jumped off I decided that it would be best of we left the city but still be close enough to carry out the rest of my plan.

See Drew was a sucker for me. Anything I wanted he made sure I got. I may not have carried his last name but you better believe that I was wifey. Of course I knew about all of the other women but I was secure with mine and knew how to play my position. So at the end of the day I was getting what was owed to me.

Drew was so set on getting his hands on that money Jewel had that he was blinded by what I was doing and who I was doing it with. But just like Adam and Eve when they were in the garden, everyone's eyes would soon be opened and the site before them would leave everyone speechless.

Double checking to make sure I had everything packed up before Drew got back I walked over and glanced in the mirror. My creamy brown complexion and dark colored contacts gave me somewhat a mysterious look or maybe it was just my imagination. The plastic surgery had done wonders for my face and body though and every man I came in contact with let it be known. Buffy the Body didn't have a thing on me I thought as I smiled to myself.

That smile slowly faded as I rubbed my hand down my stomach. The pain and the anger I felt so deep down in my being on days like this was unbearable. No woman should have to ever feel the way that I did especially at the hands of the man that she had loved. That was ok though, all would be well soon enough.

Just as I was looking down at my watch to see what time it was I heard the door beep indicating Drew was back. I had no idea where he had gone but he knew that we were on a time limit. I was beginning to worry because it would only be a matter of time before police were everywhere and letting the public know there was a missing child. Considering I hadn't received one of those Amber Alert text that normally came through and scaring the life out of me at three in the morning I knew that we were ok for the time being. He just needed to come on.

As soon as Drew walked in with a watery eyed little girl a smile so wide spread across my face. I was in here looking like the Grinch who stole Christmas! I told Drew that he needed to get me my money by any means necessary and looking into this little girl's face let me know he was on his job. I can’t lie and say that I wasn’t worried he could pull this off. Drew put off like he had it all together on the outside but he could be as dumb as a bag of rocks at times when it came to women.

That’s exactly how he got caught and didn’t even know it. Put a bad broad in front of him and he lost his fool mind. You would think that after all of these years speaking and teaching the gospel something would have eventually resonated in his spirit and he would turn from his wicked ways. Who am I kidding God didn’t care nothing about anyone but Himself. If He did I wouldn’t have been at this place that I am right now. Oh well this money that I was about to get would do me just fine and replace the Almighty.

"How did you pull this one off?" I wanted to know. This entire plan was mastermind by me so to see him taking the lead right now was doing something to me. It excited me and the rush I felt couldn't be explained.

"I knew that Jewel hadn't made the changes to would could check her out of school so I used that to my advantage. By it being the last day of school it didn't matter that I got her early." He said beaming as Kammy sat on the bed still crying.

Turning my nose up at the little girl I rolled my eyes. I hated a crying child. She was way too pretty to be making those ugly faces. Her long thick hair was pulled back into two long twisted ponytails with ribbons tied around the top and barrettes on the ends. I knew her mother had a time washing and combing all of that on the regular. She had beautiful chocolate skin and the prettiest eyes I had ever seen. Kammy looked nothing like Drew and I don't see how his behind never had a clue she wasn't his. Ray Charles knew it so why didn't he? That's what I meant when I called him dumb.

"Come on we need to get this show on the road then because it will only be a matter of time before the news is reporting this and we need to be long gone." I told him getting our things together. We had a secret hiding place that I knew only one other person knew about and she was sure to be dead by now.

Before we could get out of the room good my phone rang. Not noticing the number I decided to answer anyway. Once I finished this call I was leaving this phone right here because the last thing we needed was for someone to track us down by the signal bouncing off of a tower. I had already cleared out all of the information and reset it back to its factory settings

“Hello?” I said trying to disguise my voice a tad bit.

“Sis I messed up. I messed up so bad.”

I pulled the phone away from my ear and looked at it. I knew this wasn’t who I thought it was. See this is exactly why I liked to work alone. Someone was always messing up or getting in their feelings at the worst times.

Placing the phone back to my ear I let it rip.

"Messed up is right! I shouldn't even be talking to you right now. Did you do what I told you to do? I guess not because here I am holding a conversation with you." I was fuming mad.

This could very well be the cause of all of our demise and all because my stupid sister didn't know how to follow simple directions.

For as long as I can remember she had been the one to mess up and I had to get us out of it. She never could do anything right. That's exactly why our mother treated her the way that she did. I was now starting to understand why she got cut off and now it was my turn to let her go. I was done trying to be her savior and stand in the gap for her.

She thought that I didn't know what she was up to when she diverted from the original plan for her own gain but I was always one step ahead. My sister was good for nothing and hearing that all of her life you would think that she would try and get it together. I'm guessing it fell on deaf ears.

"I shouldn't have done this to begin with. I know this is God's way of punishing me for everything." She whined. I hated when she did that.

"Well this is one whippin you gonna take by yourself because I'm done." I told her.

"Please sis I need you! I don't have anyone else." She pleaded.

I hung up the phone not even bothering with giving a reply as Drew looked on with eyes full of questions.

“We gotta go now.” I said opening the door to the room and looking out to make sure the coast was clear.

Without a single word Drew followed behind me as we made our way to the back parking lot to the car. I had to think of something quick because if we weren’t careful the death that my sister Jasmine and her son should have been experiencing was going to fall on me.

Drew

I kept looking in the rearview mirror at Kammy and noticed she had finally fallen asleep. I knew that God didn't want to hear a thing from me but I prayed that she would be quiet because Constance couldn't stand a wining child and that's all that she had been doing since she found out she wasn't going home to her mother.

Putting my eyes back on the road I wondered where we were heading. The destination that we had planned was cancelled and I still didn't know why. When Constance got that phone call back at the room she was dead set on changing our initial plans and going for her plan B.

“Where are we going?” I asked. I found myself starting to get frustrated not knowing what was going on but the love I had for this woman canceled out everything I was feeling.

Since the day that I met her it had all been about making her happy and if I had to cause others pain just to make sure a smile was always on her face then so be it. Constance and I met on one of my many ministry trips out of town. I knew that when she walked into the church that I had to have her and when she made sure to be first in line to sow a seed into this guest speaker I knew she was thinking the same thing that I was.

That night sealed the deal as I lay in her bed and let her have her way with me. I was so into her that every time we were intimate it felt so familiar.

Like I had been in her forbidden garden before. It just felt so right and the more I was with her the deeper I fell in love with her. I knew that once we got this money we would go off and get married and be the family that I wanted to have. Everything I did I did for her and our two children.

Thinking of our children I wondered where they were. As strange as it may sound I had yet to lay my eyes on the two of them in person since they have been in this world. When Constance told me that she had gone into labor a little over a year ago I was out of the country and by the time I got back my situation at home wouldn't allow me the time to get away again so soon. It was like every time I was available Constance wasn't or vice versa.

By the time I did see her, her body had snapped back like she hadn't even had a set of twins. When I asked her why she didn't bring the kids with her she told me that her mother had them and she wanted to spend some alone time with me. Who was I to deny my queen her request? A smile crept up on my face as I thought about us finally being a family. A rich family at that.

I glanced over at Constance as she pulled out one of the burner phones she had purchased.

"Pull over up here." Was all she said.

We had just made it on the other side of Anderson, South Carolina and there was a rest stop coming into view. I wasn't comfortable pulling over just yet being that we weren't far enough down I-85 and it was still light out. We hadn't heard anything yet about Kammy's kidnapping on the scanner we had with us. I knew that it was only a matter of time before everyone would be on high alert and the last thing I needed was for someone to recognize us before we could get to where we were going.

"I don't think this is a good idea." I said voicing my concern while looking in my rearview.

"Why not? No one knows we have her and by the time they find out we will be long gone." She said to me.

The look on my face told her that something was wrong and I had hoped she wouldn't ask me right now. I had messed up and the last thing I wanted was for her to lay into me right now.

"Look the faster you pull over so we can make this call the faster we can get back on the road. We need to do whatever we can for them not to suspect that we are behind this." She said with not an ounce of worry in her voice.

Doing as she said I let off of the gas and started making my way to the back of the rest area where the trees were thick and part of the building hid us from view. I knew I was going to have to tell her my mess up sooner or later but I would hold out as long as I could.

"Here call Jewel and let her know what we want and that she has until tomorrow morning to deposit the money into this Paypal account." Constance said firing off instructions while passing me the phone.

I guess it was going to be sooner but I couldn't bring myself to do it right now.

I checked to see if Kammy was still asleep because the last thing I needed was for her to wake up and make any kind of noise. She was a smart six year old and her mother had always taught her what to do if she was ever taken. That's why I needed her to remain asleep for now.

Putting the phone to my ear I waited for someone to answer.

"Speaker." Constance said with a look on her face that said she didn't trust me to handle this right.

Doing as I was told we waited.

"Hello! Drew is that you where is my baby Drew?" Jewel yelled on the other end of the phone.

Before I could respond I saw the look that Constance was giving me letting me know that she knew I had messed up.

I was only supposed to grab Kammy once she came out of the school and just head to Rock Hill. Instead I went inside of the school like I normally would and checked her out. I knew that no one would be alarmed because everyone was familiar with me. That should have been even more of a reason to stick to what Constance said do. Figuring if I waited until school was out there was a chance that Jewel or Bryce would be there to get Kammy and I couldn't risk not showing up without her.

The only reason I let Kammy call Jewel in the first place was because I figured it would buy us some time. I let my pride get in the way of the plan and this may have cost us everything.

The pride before the plan. What a powerful statement. I thought about how all along we can know the plan that God has set before us to follow but we let our pride come before it all and want to do things our way. Nothing ever comes out right when we do that but time and time again we try and take over. I knew it was my pride that got the best of me when I found out about how Bryce felt about Jewel.

She wasn't supposed to be my wife and I knew it. Oddly enough God had shown me over and over that she didn't belong to me but I didn't care. Andrew Webber was the man and I was going to get what I wanted by any means necessary.

"What did you do?" she mouthed to me. Instead of responding to Constance I read off what was on the paper she had handed me.

"If you want what's best for Kammy I suggest you get prepared to deposit that inheritance into my account. I'll call you back in two days to give you the rest of the information that you will need in order to do that." I said into the receiver. Constance wanted to hold off on giving the instructions right away in order to receive the money and I didn't understand why. This was the whole reason that we kidnapped Kammy in the first place so that we could get that money and leave. I was in no position to question her right now though after I messed up so I decided to just keep quiet.

Because Jewel knew that I had Kammy I knew she wasn't shocked by the sound of my voice. The device Constance had over the mouth piece altered my voice to sound robotic but it was all for nothing.

"Drew I know it's you since you already let Kammy call me. Please don't hurt our baby!" Jewel cried out. Just that fast I forgot that I was supposed to be trying to remain anonymous even if I had messed up already. But hearing Jewel saying *our* baby did something to me. I knew she wasn't referring to her being our daughter together but she was talking about her and Bryce being Kammy's parents.

"Our baby? Our baby! Who's baby Jewel? You mean you and Bryce's child!" I started yelling before Constance snatched the phone from me throwing it out of the window.

"Fool! Drive! You can't do nothing right! Messing around with you gonna get us caught." Constance fumed as I put the car into gear and got back on the highway.

I knew she was mad and I couldn't blame her. I let my emotions get the best of me in that moment and I could possibly risk us getting caught.

"I'm sorry bab-." She said cutting me off by throwing her hand in my face.

"You got that right you're sorry. From now on just do as I say. I can't believe that you called her and gave them a heads up. See this is why I'm glad I always have another plan."

Pulling out another phone I saw her pull up a map and study it for a minute before telling me to turn around on the next exit. I didn't know what we were doing but considering the way I just screwed up I was letting her run the show. I just hoped the feeling in my gut wasn't an indication of what lied ahead for us.

Kammy

I listened to my first daddy yelling at my mommy and I just wanted to go home. The way that lady with him looked at me scared me. She was so pretty but she was so mean at the same time.

My daddy Bryce wouldn't let anyone talk to me like she does if he was here. I was scared to open my eyes to see where we were because I didn't want them to fuss at me anymore. If me wanting to go to Disney World was causing all of these problems then I don't want to go anymore.

God please take me home to my mommy, my daddy, and my sister. I miss them so much.

Mommy said that whenever I feel scared about anything that I should talk to you. I'm a big girl but I'm so scared God. What if they hurt me? I didn't know money was so important and made people do crazy stuff. If that's what happens then I don't want any when I grow up.

God will you tell mommy that I'm ok please? I don't want them to worry about me. Sometimes she gets in her bed for days when she is real stressed and I don't want her to do that anymore. Please help me. I promise I will be a good girl all of the time and not just when I want something. I will even be nice to the kids that are mean to me at school. Amen.

The car stopped and I felt the door open and me being snatched out of the seat. I dared not to open my eyes as we moved along. I stayed as still as I could like I do on Christmas Eve when I have to act like I'm sleeping before Santa comes.

Hurry God. Please hurry!

Jewel

Thinking to myself this was all my fault as I listened to the techs and detectives trying to work as fast as they could to trace the phone that Drew had just used. For a minute I thought that he had passed her off to someone else and they had my baby because I didn't recognize the voice but as soon as I spoke about Kammy he flipped. That's when I knew that it was him. Hearing me call her our daughter triggered something inside of him as well as within me.

I was positive that this was my punishment for all of the wrong I had done when it came to the relationship I shared with Bryce. I knew that when we conceived Avery I should have been truthful and made things right, maybe I wouldn't be in this predicament right now had I done right. But I was so ashamed and confused about what I was doing I just wanted it to all go away.

The first time could have been looked at as a mistake but the second time Bryce and I fell to temptation was no mistake. My heart was with Bryce and we both knew it. I felt like so did our parents but no one ever said a thing about it. I guess they wanted to see how we would fix it. So many nights I lay beside Drew thinking of the man that held my heart and I prayed that God would take the feeling away but He never did. The older we got and the more distant Drew became I felt that I needed to make it right with the man that I shared vows with.

So I backed away from Bryce and only interacted with him if something needed to be done with the ministry. It took a while but he finally picked up on my vibes and respected my feelings. That was another thing that made me love him. No matter what he was attentive to my feelings instead of his own unlike Drew who only cared about himself and what he could get.

All I could think about was that this had to be my punishment for the life I lived and I just wished that God would make me pay some other way. I would gladly trade my own life for my daughter's if that meant she would be returned to us unharmed. I had been fighting that feeling in the pit of my stomach since I received the first phone call from Kammy earlier in the day. That feeling that was telling me to go up to my medicine cabinet, reach behind all of the over the counter cold medicines, and grab that bottle of prescription pain killers. It had been a long time since I've gone down that road but I felt like it was time for me to take a trip down memory lane.

When I ended up in the hospital after I found out about Drew's secret life with other women that was the first time that I tried to take my own life. Everyone thought it was because I had recently miscarried and I was finding it hard to deal with. No one but Bryce knew the truth and when my husband should have been there with me he was out with one of his many mistresses. The pain I felt was unbearable but the embarrassment I felt not being able to keep my husband out of the arms of another woman consumed me. I figured if I had been what he wanted then he wouldn't need anyone else, I wouldn't have caught him with someone in his office, and our son would still be alive. It was because of me that lives were being destroyed and taken from me. This was my punishment.

"Come on baby calm down. You can't get yourself worked up like this." My mother said wrapping her arms around me.

"It's all my fault mommy." I cried into her shoulder.

"Shhh. Don't do this to yourself baby. We've all made mistakes and as long as we repent and turn from our wicked ways God is a forgiving God." She said trying her best to comfort me. I knew what she was saying was true but what about when my wicked ways involved the man who held my heart? I had long ago fell out of love with Drew but I didn't want to disappoint my family, our church, and most importantly God.

Before I had a chance to ask her anything else there was a lot of commotion coming from our dining room where the police had set up all of their equipment.

"We got a trace!" I heard the tech call out as everyone rushed over to see what he was looking at. Although the phone that Drew called me from was a burner phone and not registered to anyone it still had to use a cell phone tower. They were able to get the location of the nearest tower which was close to a rest area on I-85 in Anderson, South Carolina.

It took a while but they were finally able to get a patrol car dispatched to the location. Being that rest stops were very popular for truck drivers it didn't take long to find a couple of drivers that had been there a while who remembered seeing a dark blue SUV stop then speed off only moments later. That could have been anyone and if it wasn't for Kammy's school giving a description of the car that Drew picked her up in it may have been a dead end. At least we had an area of where they many have been and that was a start. If God didn't bring my baby home to us safely the next time I may succeed in ending my own pain.

Constance

Drew was working my nerves. It was like when he was still with Jewel he was focused but now that he was with me full time and we had that wining child with us he was off his game.

When I found out this fool had called Jewel and let her know he had Kammy I was livid! I knew that I had to take things into my own hands if I wanted to see any of this money and get the payback that I needed. Had I not been prepared Drew would have gotten us hemmed up. It was a reason I had him go down 85 and stop at that rest area. It was the quickest route to where I had planned for us to go but it was also an area that I knew well. I was able to make sure that just in case anything happened and the police were on to us we would be able to avoid them.

I had my mother rent a car in her name and drop it off exactly where I told her. We were just getting back on the highway heading in the other direction when I saw the blue lights flashing on the other side of the road heading to the rest area we had just left. Looking over at Drew I didn't say a word as I slid a cd in the player and turned it up. It was time to get to this money and unlike Drew I wasn't going to con the good church folks with a flamboyant sermon about blessings and prosperity that I knew would never come. Waka Flocka had just amped me up as I picked up speed and sang along, 'Yeaaaahhhhhh oh let's do it!"

****

Walking into work the next day like everything was normal was a piece of cake. No one would ever know what was going on with me because I never associated with too many people. I came in daily with my professional and friendly attitude just like the next person. There were only a select few that I let inside my circle but once they were done serving their purpose I cut them off. I knew it was only a matter of time before I had to get ghost once again but before I did these loose ends needed to be tied up.

"Good morning boo!" I said putting on my lab coat and getting ready to start my day.

"Hey love. How did you enjoy your two days off?" My coworker Samantha asked me.

I liked Sammie as she liked to be called. She was real down to earth but she still had that hood side I could relate to. Whenever I did decide to go out on the town she was my go to girl. When I first met her I was a little apprehensive of the biracial woman. I knew she wasn't all the way black but she didn't look all the way white to me either. She had a body of a goddess though so I knew somewhere down the line she had some black in her. But what really sealed the deal was when she opened her mouth. Mama was straight outta the hood!

"Girl it was a little rough." I said beginning my sob story. I needed Sammie to be able to lie for me unknowingly just in case them boys in blue showed up asking questions. And if she didn't cooperate? Let's just say that she wouldn't want the little secret that she thought no one knew about her to come to light. See everything I do is calculated and meticulous and I always have a backup plan.

"Why what happened boo?" she asked with her voice filled with concern.

"You know I went to Memphis to see my mom. I knew she was sick but when I got there she was so much worse than I had anticipated." I lied straight through my pearly whites. I was even able to scrap up a few tears to add to my performance.

"Aww boo I'm so sorry." She said walking over to me. "Is there anything I can do for you?" She asked just like I knew she would.

"The only thing is that I need is someone to watch my little sister for a while. I have to work in order to help my mother pay for her medical bills. I can't miss work. I took a chance at taking two days off so that I could go see about her." I was really letting the waterworks fly on the outside but on the inside I was cracking up. I should have really been an actress.

"Hold on let me work something out for you. My aunt works from home so she shouldn't mind helping out. Let me call her on my break and I will let you know ok? Don't cry Connie I got you boo." She said calling me by that awful nickname. I had told this wanch we were not the wonder twins and to stop calling me that but I decided to let her slide this time.

"Thank you so much Sammie. Let me go get myself together before anyone sees me." I said walking off towards the restroom. Once I got inside I pulled out my phone and sent a text.

Me: It's a go!

Bae: Already!

Me: How long will this take?

Bae: Once I put everything in place and run the labs it will take no longer than a week.

Me: Bet! <3

See what Drew failed to realize was that he wasn't my one and only. While he should have been living out the word of God and being the husband his wife deserved he let his personal desires take over. He had always been that way for as long as I remembered. Especially back in high school.

Oh that's right y'all don't know our back history huh? You thought this was a new fling between him and me? Well join the club because so did he. Confused? Let me help you out then. Grab that tea cup cause this here is hot or do you prefer a little communion wine?

****

20 Years Ago…

I hated the way I looked. My body hadn't realized that I was almost grown because it still looked like an 8th grader's body. My hair was real short and unmanageable, the braces I wore made my mouth look bigger than it actually was, and while all of the other girls were sporting real bras I was had a bra that was trying to train something that wasn't there at all.

It was like none of the boys paid me any mind and the only friend I had was my sister. Our mother Regina raised us alone and while I thought Jasmine was the prettier of us two, our mother made it seem like I was the beauty queen of the family. Some days I would feel bad at how she treated Jasmine. I just figured it was because she hated Jasmine's father, or maybe because she didn't know who he was. My father was her first love but he passed away from an unknown illness when I was three.

Jasmine never showed on the outside that she was bothered by the things my mother said to her. She would put a smile on her face and keep it moving. Her grades excelled because she was determined to make it out of this house. But there were so many nights that she would come into my room and cry about the hurtful things our mother would say to her.

There were days that I often got mad at Jasmine because she was ungrateful to me. Her beauty attracted all of the boys in her middle school and I wanted to be looked at like that. It didn't matter that my mother told me she couldn't please me like I thought I should be pleased.

So when Drew approached me, instead of me being cautious I was all in from the jump. See everyone at school knew me as Camilla Ropier. It wasn't until I got older that I decided to change my name in order to get payback from the person that caused me the most pain.

I thought the day that Drew came smiling in my face he was really interested. I was so naive and dumb back then. I partially blamed my mother because had she been truthful towards me when he came hollering about me being cute and beautiful I would have known he was lying. Instead I let him gas me up and before I knew it I was giving up the only thing that I really had that made me beautiful in God's eyes. Once that was gone I knew that I was tainted.

It wasn't until I saw those two pink lines on a pregnancy three months later that I knew my life would never be the same. Initially I was ecstatic and so was my mother. Even Jasmine couldn't wait to be an aunt. I just knew that my mom would be upset with me but when I told her who the father was she immediately saw dollar signs.

Drew wasn't rich by a long shot but he was well on his way to the pros. For that fact alone she suggested I waited until I got a little further along before telling him. That way he couldn't force me to get an abortion. Little did either of us know that come hell or high water Drew was going to make me lose my baby one way or another.

I had just reached four months and now was the time to tell Drew. Since he was a year ahead of me in school he would be graduating in a couple of months and I wanted him to be aware of his child. My mother had me so hype with what she thought he was going to say, that I didn't think about the negative.

Walking into the cafeteria that fateful day I had my sonogram in hand and a smile a mile wide on my face. Drew was sitting with his boys chatting it up and instead of pulling him aside like something told me to I decided to make our announcement a public one.

"Hey Drew." I said waiting for his excitement to match mine. That never happened thought.

"Wassup?" he said as if I was bothering him. I noticed his best friend Bryce shaking his head as the other guys tried to hold in their laughter.

"I have a surprise for you." I told him standing there looking like who done it and why.

Mama thought that I should fix myself up when I told him about the baby so she tried her best to straighten and curl my hair, she let me wear one of her dresses that was a tad bit too big, and some kitten heels that almost took me out earlier when I was coming down the steps. You couldn't tell me I wasn't fly but by the looks on Drew's face he thought otherwise.

"A surprise?" He asked with an arched eyebrow.

"Yeah. Here." I handed him the sonogram as the table of guys erupted.

"Yoooooooo Drew you got the mark pregnant?" his friend Alex laughed with tears in his eyes.

Mark? What did he mean by mark?

I guess my face showed my confusion because Drew stood up and walked over to me. My silly behind thought he was about to say something comforting like what my mother had envisioned but she was wrong yet again.

"If that's my baby then you need to get rid of it. You were just a mark. Somebody that we knew would be an easy lay and you gave it up just like I thought. I appreciate that come up though. Because of you I was able to make these fools come up off of a few dollars." He fell out laughing while dapping his boys up.

The tears were falling faster than I could wipe them away. I didn't know why I let my mother and my feelings deceive me. Drew and I only had sex once and I should have known there was no way that he was in love with me the way I was with him. My aunt told me once that the Bible says never be anxious about anything but in everything we do be prayerful and thankful as we let our request be known to God. I think it went something like that. It didn't matter now though because the way I was being treated even if I did pray God wouldn't have heard it anyway.

"I'm keeping my baby." I said just above a whisper right before he could get too far away from me causing him to stop in his tracks.

"Excuse me?" He asked walking back over and putting his hand up to his ear like he was trying to make sure he heard me correctly.

"I said I'm keeping my baby. Our baby!" I yelled getting the attention of everyone in the cafeteria.

This seemed to only make him even more furious now that others outside of his crew knew our secret. Instead of saying anything else he looked at me with so much malice and hatred in his eyes that I knew nothing good would come out of this like my mother had told me. Once again she had lied and it caused me to miss all of the signs I needed in order to make the right choice.

For the next week it seemed like all eyes were on me no matter where I went around school.

The day I told Drew about the baby I went home to fill my mother and sister in. Can you believe she didn't have not once single comforting word to give to me? It was like I was on my own with that and she knew that she had made the wrong decision by making me tell him.

One day after school I decided to take the short cut home. I was almost six months pregnant and by me being so small my son felt like he was weighing me down. I could no longer take my normal route and against my better judgement I took the back way home. I was just about to the area where our apartments would come into view when out of nowhere three girls that I had never seen before jumped out on me. They beat me so long and so bad that it took me a while to get to where someone would see me.

The thing that stuck out to me was when one of them mentioned Drew and the baby. My ears were ringing so bad that those were the only two words that I could make out before they ran off. It was in that moment that I knew this was all his doing and my heart instantly became cold.

Hours passed before someone noticed me and the doctor said that once I got to the hospital had it been any longer I would have died along with my baby. When I heard that I knew that this was all Drew's doing. He knew I couldn't get an abortion because I was too far along so he had someone else give me one instead. That was the day that I made up in mind that come hell or high water Andrew Webber would pay for the pain he caused me by any means necessary.

***

I took my hands and placed them under the faucet so that I could wash my face. Thinking back on those memories always felt like I was reliving the past and no matter how hard I tried I couldn't stop crying. Reaching over to the paper towel dispenser I looked in the mirror as I wiped my face and removing the makeup that I had covering my scars.

See when those girls beat me like they did they beat me so bad that I was almost unrecognizable. I had to have a few reconstructive surgeries to repair my nose that was almost crushed along with my jaw needing a plate in it.

Because of this it altered my appearance and once my body finally decided to develop, I looked like a totally different person.

I was thrown off when after I was released from the hospital that my mother had packed up all of our stuff and we were leaving the state. I had no idea that she was going to leave Jasmine behind. What kind of mother would just leave their child with nothing but I couldn't focus on that too long. I had to get well because I was going to make sure that Drew eventually paid for hurting me.

It wasn't long after leaving that I was able to get word about how he went off to college and had my grades been good enough to get into a school closer to him I would have. I thought all hope was lost that is until I decided to come back home to visit Jasmine and she told me she had gotten accepted into Spelman. I anticipated our relationship was going to be really rocky instead she was just excited to have me there with her again. It had been years since I saw her and once we left my mother never mentioned her at all. As soon as she told me the school she got into I knew she would be my partner in crime. The only thing I was worried about was that if Jasmine helped me to get my payback Drew would recognize me once he saw me again. That fear was soon out the door when he finally did see me. He was so blinded by my body that it never crossed his mind I was Camilla. What I didn't plan on though was for Jasmine to fall in love with my mark.

Walking back into the lab I put my past in the back of my mind and focused on the next thing that I needed to do in order to get this ball rolling. Soon and very soon Drew will be reaping what he has sown and I will have exactly what I needed to be living the life that I deserved.

Jewel

Nothing in this world could have ever prepared me for a time such as this. Whenever I hear news reports on abducted children I always thought this couldn't happen to me and my family. Never in a million years did I ever see Drew stooping this low just to hurt us but money made people do crazy things. It had been a little over a week and we still haven't heard anything else from Drew.

I remember hearing during one of the sermons a guest speaker gave. Apostle Carlos White said that people will always say what they won't do in a situation if it ever happened to them but just as soon as the situation presents itself to them their thought process changed.

Like the Prodigal son when he was so down and out that even the food he fed the pigs looked good to him. He never would have thought he would be so hungry to where that would be his reality until he was in it. I guess Drew was so desperate for that payout he would go to any lengths to get what it was he wanted. Even if it was something that he never thought he would do.

Thinking back on the beginning of my relationship with Drew I realized just how blinded I was from what was really going on around me. My parents raised me and my brother Chris with so much love and a solid foundation in Christ that there should have been no way that I ended up going down the road that I was on. I was searching for the love of a man all because another one hurt me so deep.

Usually we hear about women who settled for no good men because of them having daddy issues but that couldn't have been further from the truth. My dad was a wonderful man. He was kind, loving, and such an awesome provider. He made sure to lead his family in the way that God had ordained him to.

When I fell in love with Romeo I just knew that he was the one. He was going to treat me just like my father treated my mother. As soon as he broke my heart I was in search of the next man to give me what it was I was searching for and although I felt in my heart that Drew really wasn't it he was close enough. That was until I started coming around Bryce.

Just the thought of him made me smile and I knew that I had made a big mistake in getting into a relationship with Drew. At the time Drew and I were courting and I told him about my past, he did everything that I thought he should be doing in order to capture my heart. On the outside we looked like the perfect couple but on the inside I knew that this wasn't right.

He appeared to show everyone just how much he loved me and that's what did it for me. Romeo was ashamed of me and wanted to hide us until he got what he wanted but Drew was open with everything he was doing. After a while I got comfortable and turned a blind eye to what I knew God was telling me.

The night Bryce and I intertwined our souls was like nothing I had ever experienced before. I didn't feel anything close to what I felt with him each time Drew and I were intimate. After that night neither of us mentioned it again until Avery was born. One look at her and I knew that she was the product of my affair and Bryce knew it as well. Right before I was about to break it off with Drew and tell him what had happened he proposed right there in my hospital room.

With my parents giving him their blessing and Bryce looking like he was already defeated I accepted. God knows I wish I would have been strong enough to walk away but I wasn't. Once everyone left that evening I prayed and prayed. I asked God to forgive me for everything I've done and to please give me peace with my decision. I vowed to be the wife that Drew deserved because he was such a loving man to me. But once those vows were said it was a wrap.

The first five years of our marriage we were in marital bliss. Drew was so loving and attentive to both Avery and I. It was strange though because once Avery was born she never wanted to be around Drew no matter how hard he tried. It was like she knew something that I didn't. I brushed it off though as her just being a mama's girl.

By the time our sixth wedding anniversary came around things had drastically changed. No longer did he want us traveling with him out of town when he had to speak at different seminars and churches. The look in his eyes were starting to show me that he wasn't really into this anymore and I couldn't understand why. Still I brushed it off and went harder for my man than ever before. I was not about to lose this man that I loved like I did Romeo. I was determined to have that longevity in my marriage like my parents.

The day I found out about the other women I was heartbroken and ashamed. And who was there just like before? Bryce. Even after I broke his heart by marrying Drew and let him believe he was Avery's father, he was still there for me. I know it looks bad being a married woman as well as a first lady but in my heart I knew that I had married the wrong man. I just couldn't get out of it and somewhere in me at the time I didn't want to.

Bryce had plenty of opportunities to tell me what Drew was doing behind my back but he didn't. He felt that would be like him causing trouble for Drew just so that I would leave him. He wanted me to seek God and prayed that my eyes were opened on their own. That way no one could say that he was the reason. Even for a while after I found out what Drew was up to Bryce kept his distance. He could have very well influenced my decision to leave Drew sooner but he chose not to.

One night when Drew was on yet another mission trip out of the country Bryce came by the house to check on us. Avery was eleven at the time and she knew something in our home wasn't right but she never asked any questions. She stayed in a child's place. I knew that Drew wasn't really doing the work of the Lord this trip and I had gone into a bit of a funk.

Avery had just gone to my parent's house for the weekend and Bryce stopped by to give me some of the information I needed for an upcoming conference. As soon as I let him in my personal space feelings for him resurfaced. This was the first time in years that I had this feeling around him. I didn't know if it was because of the information I had recently found out about my husband or if it was because the love and attraction for him was once again staring me in my face. Either way I felt like this was going to end wrong.

“Hey J.” He said with a solemn expression across his face. I didn’t know if he was upset, tired, frustrated or what. But I did know that he wasn’t really himself.

“Hey Bryce. Come in are you ok?” I asked him closing the door behind him and making my way back to the kitchen.

I never felt like I had to hide anything from Bryce and I could be myself so when I entered the kitchen I went right back over to the Hennessy bottle I had stashed for a rainy day. I knew drinking wouldn’t solve my issues and it was frowned upon by many Christians, especially with me being a First Lady, but I didn’t care about all of that. I just wanted to numb the pain.

Walking over to me Bryce just stood there for a moment before saying anything.

“You gonna pour me one or do I have to take the whole bottle for myself?” He said making me think he was joking.

Just as soon as the smile appeared on my face it left. Bryce didn’t drink and the times he did there was something seriously going on.

“Are you ok?” I asked ignoring his request for a drink and walking around the counter to him.

“No I’m not ok J. This is killing me knowing that each night I go home to an empty house while the woman who is to be my wife is laid up with a man that is only with her under false pretenses.” He fumed. Bryce wasn’t yelling at me but I could hear the anger in his voice as he spoke.

I remained quiet because I honestly didn't know what to say. I understood exactly where Bryce was coming from and why. God will never send someone else's husband or wife to be with another person but what if the person they married wasn't who they were supposed to be with in the first place? Like knowing you heard God tell you not to marry that person just as clear as day but you allowed your flesh and what you wanted to get in the way of that. God had spoken to me as if He was standing in front of my face telling me to leave Drew alone but I was hardheaded and now not only were my girls and I suffering but so was the man I should have married.

Ushering Bryce into our den we sat together on my couch throwing back drink after drink. I listened to him as he poured his heart out to me before finally telling me that he loved me. As soon as those three words left his mouth and met my ears I knew this was really where I should have been. God knows that this man held my heart but I knew it was so wrong of me to be feeling like this towards anyone that wasn't my husband but it felt so right. The love I had for Bryce ached badly and I wish I had never gotten involved with Drew to begin with. Who was I kidding? I knew that what we were doing and what we felt would be frowned upon by so many people especially the good old Christians down to the church house.

While I was trying to gather my thoughts Bryce leaned over and his lips met mine for the first time in over a decade. It felt right and it felt normal and I knew it was not only because it was what my flesh wanted but I felt that my spirit needed it as well. Needless to say two months later I found out I was pregnant with Kammy.

"Mom Detective Jones just called and said he was on his way over here. He needs to show you something and Daddy just pulled up." Avery said bringing me out of my thoughts.

"Oh…um ok baby here I come." I said pulling my hair up into a high ponytail and slipping on my slides.

I made it downstairs just as Bryce was bringing in the take out he had gotten for us because cooking was not on the agenda or my to-do list these days. As soon as he made it to the kitchen the front door opened again and in walked my parents. I was surprised to see them because neither had called to let me know they were coming over.

"Hey Mommy and Daddy what are the two of you doing here?" I asked while giving them each a hug and a kiss.

"Baby I don't know I just feel like the Holy Spirit needed us to be here." My father said as Bryce came out of the kitchen. I watched how both of my parent's faces lit up when they saw him.

Each and every time they were around Bryce they were full of life and now that I looked back on everything I could never remember a time when they looked happy around Drew. My eyes had to have been so blinded to the truth all of these years. Maybe if I had seen all of this in the beginning maybe things would have been different for everybody.

I didn't really have an appetite but I knew I had to eat and just like a caring and concerned husband should be, Bryce made sure I had something on my stomach. Even with the aroma of the shrimp fried rice hitting my nostrils and my stomach calling out to the high heavens for me to fill it, I could only eat a few spoonfuls before I had had enough.

The ringing of the doorbell startled me and all of a sudden I was too nervous to open it. Something was telling me whatever was on the other side of that door waiting for us was not about to do anything but make matters worse. Since I didn't move fast enough my father headed to the front while Bryce came and stood in front of me.

"Breathe slow J." He said pulling me closer to him and rubbing both of my arms. I didn't realize that I had started to have a panic attack until he put his hands on me. Bryce was the only one who knew how to get me to calm down during these times. All Drew ever told me to do was go outside and get some fresh air.

My breathing had returned to normal just as my father and Detective Jones and his partner came through the dining room to where we were. The look on his face told me something was seriously wrong and I was scared out of my mind.

"Good afternoon everyone." He said looking around the room.

Everyone responded except me. I was too scared to utter a word so I just nodded my head.

Clearing his throat he placed his hand into his pocket and pulled out a small manila envelope that contained a red evidence label across it. At that moment my world felt like it was slowing down and the sounds around me began to sound muffled. The heat in the room must have been turned up because I was starting to sweat and felt hot all over.

I saw Detective Jones' lips moving but his words were not coherent at the moment. I watched the look of sheer horror hit my mother's face before she broke down in my father's arms. His face was now wet as well as Bryce and Avery's while he held on to our daughter.

The moment when everything became clear to me was when the detective opened up the envelope and removed its contents. The cute little charm bracelet that I had gotten Kammy on her birthday was melted. All except the little bunny charm that stood out with Kammy's birthstone as its eye.

"I'm so sorry Mrs. Webber but this was the only thing we could use to identify your daughter. Because of the condition of her body being burned as bad as it was, the description that you gave us of what she was wearing the day that she was taken helped us be able to identify her." He said as my world went black.

Avery

Waiting for my mother to come to, I sat on the side of her hospital bed and twirled the engagement ring that James had given me a few of weeks ago. I still couldn't believe that he and I were getting married but I knew he was the one. It was just sad that I couldn't even enjoy the excitement from it all because we had just received the news that my little sister was no longer here.

As soon as the detective told us what happened and showed us the evidence they had it felt like our whole world had ended. Mommy was so hysterical that we had to call the ambulance to come and see about her. She was uncontrollable and we all understood why she was responding like she did. No parent should have to bury their children but it should be the children burying their parents only after they have lived a fulfilling life.

We had been in the hospital for the last couple of days and each time she came out of her slumber and reality hit her she was wilding out again. It hurt me so bad to see her going through this and not be able to do anything for her. She was sinking deeper and deeper into that desolate place and my biggest fear was that she wouldn't come back out.

My phone vibrated in my pocket and a slight smile etched across my weary face as I looked at the picture James and I took at my graduation flash on the screen. I didn't know how he did it but every time I was going through something he would call me at the right time. It felt like he was right here instead of being in Georgia.

Not long after we received the news about my sister he called. I was unable to talk to him because I was so distraught but my Uncle Chris took the call and then placed it on speaker so that I could hear him praying for us all. This was why I loved him so much.

“Hey love.” I said answering the phone. I walked over to the window so that I wouldn’t disturb mommy while she was sleeping. She had had a rough night and morning so I knew she needed all of the rest she could get.

“Hey beautiful. You alright?” He asked me with genuine concern.

"Just worried about mommy and trying to deal with my baby sister being gone. It's too much you know?" I said before I began to cry.

"Aww man I hate to hear you cry and I'm not there with you. I'm so sorry that yall are going through this. Listen I'm not going to preach or go into a long prayer or anything but I want you to know that God is still in control. Don't stop trusting Him. I don't know but I feel like something is off with all of this." He said.

"What do you mean off?" I asked once I was able to get myself together. If you asked me everything was off in my life right now and I was waiting on God to show up and turn it back on.

"I don't know. I mean if they were wanting money why didn't they ever call back with the information needed to pay the ransom? Didn't you say that's what was supposed to happen?" He wanted to know.

I thought about what James had said and he was right. We never got the call back as promised and once they found the car with no trace of either Drew or Kammy we didn't hear anything else.

If it wasn't my mother or Bryce calling Detective Jones asking questions then no one was saying anything. All he kept saying was that they were looking into every lead possible and he had no doubt that they would call again for the money.

"You're right. They just keep telling us though that hopefully their delay in calling would give the police enough time to try and track them down. Why what are you thinking?" I asked. He definitely had my attention and he was sounding more and more like his grandfather Rob who was a retired detective.

"You sure you are going to be an engineer because you are sounding like a Criminal Justice major right about now." I said before he could answer my last question.

"I think I been around Grandpa Rob too much lately." He chuckled. His grandmother Mary had finally reunited with her first love who was now a retired detective. They had been spending a lot of time together in preparation for him going off to college.

"I know bae it's crazy but something just doesn't sound right to me. Why do that to lil sis without even securing the money that was asked for first?" James asked.

Nothing made sense to me these days so I didn't even know how to answer that question. Before we could go any further mommy started stirring in her sleep.

"Hey bae she's waking up. Let me make sure she's ok and I'll call you right back ok?" I said to him. James agreed and before he hung up he made sure to say a quick prayer of covering for us and ended the call. That was something else that I loved about him. James made sure that we never hung up without a quick prayer and I could only imagine the type of husband he would be for me the more he grew closer to Christ.

"KAMMY! KAMMY!" My mother screamed out.

I rushed over to her letting her know I was there and pressing the nurse's button at the same time. It was like she wasn't aware of anything anymore except that her baby was gone. I didn't know how to help her and all I could do was watch as the nurses rushed in and put something in her IV that made her go right back out as I began to pray.

"God we need you like never before. I don't know what the lesson is in all of this but I pray that you reveal it to us in your time Lord. Please forgive us for all the wrong we have one and maybe this is us reaping what we have already sown. Only you know God. I pray that you just med our family after this terrible loss. It may seem funny for me to be at peace already but that may just be because I know you have your arms around Kammy and my mother at this very moment. Please bring peace to us all as we lay her to rest this week. Whatever you are doing in our lives I will trust you. Thank you God in advance. Amen." I prayed as I watched my beautiful mother's chest rise and fall.

Jasmine

That's right I'm still here. God knows I shouldn't be and I guess He felt like death would have been too easy for me. Instead here I am locked away in a Mecklenburg County jail cell while my precious son is laying cold in the ground.

It had been only a short time ago since I crushed those pills up in my baby's sippy cup and sent him into a cold and lonely place. I tried sending myself to that same place because unlike my mother abandoning me, I didn't want to do that to DJ but I had. Thanks to the clerk on duty at the hotel we were in, she scanned the guest's keycard for my room instead of the room next door. The older gentleman would have just backed out of the room had he not seen the pill bottles on the night stand and DJ foaming at the mouth.

By the time the police and ambulance arrived DJ was gone and I was barely holding on. Had he waited just a few more minutes to come in I wouldn't be sitting in here in a jumpsuit and having my freedom taken away from me.

I guess this would be where I blamed my mother and sister for me ending up where I was but in reality this wasn't their fault. No one knew that Constance and I were sisters. We were some years apart and as different as night and day. Constance was like the ugly duckling and here I was the prettier of the two but our mother never saw it that way.

Every time I turned around she was giving Constance compliments but being so hurtful and hateful to me. My sister tried her best to make me feel loved but sometimes I felt like she didn't care for me too much either. Only when it was convenient for her and she would gain something from it.

See when she went through her issue with Drew I was the first one she told that she was carrying his baby. I was so excited to be an aunt. The idea left just as quickly as it had come when she got jumped on by a group of girls one day walking home from school. Because of how severely she was beaten and the surgeries she had to go through my mother felt like it was best to leave the state. The only thing was I wouldn't be going with them.

I was left to fend for myself and make do with what I had. After some years later Constance came back right before I graduated high school and I told her where I was going to school at. I was determined to make my mother eat those negative words she would constantly say to me. Yea I had to do things that I wasn't proud of to make it but I got it done.

The look on her face when I told her I was about to head to Atlanta for school should have been a red flag for me but considering I was just happy to have some support I brushed it off.

The first time I saw Drew I immediately called my sister. She wasn't surprised and told me how she knew that he was in school there and needed my help with something. Drew didn't know that Constance or Camilla which was her real name, even had a little sister because I was younger than them. He couldn't even say that we resembled one another because we looked nothing alike.

At first I was all for helping her get her revenge. In a way I blamed him for causing my mother to abandon me. Had he not had Camilla beaten the way he did then they wouldn't have had to leave. It was just that I didn't expect feelings for him to cloud my judgement. I started placing the blame more on my mother and Camilla instead of Drew like my sister wanted me to.

That’s why it was so easy for me switch things up. Once I found out about Jewel and her money I felt like that would draw us closer. I didn’t think that he was playing me and no one could tell me otherwise.

Each day I could feel God telling me this wasn’t right and I knew it wouldn’t end well but I didn’t care. I had been taken advantage of my whole life and for what? To end up struggling and now I had to struggle with a kid?

No matter how many times I got pregnant by Drew I was made to get an abortion. All except this last time. I hid out until I was just about due before saying anything to either of them. I was shocked when he actually acted like he was happy about it. He wanted to know why I didn’t tell him and I explained that I thought like the other times he would make me get rid of it. I was tired of having abortion after abortion and I wanted my son. He agreed and once again had me wrapped around his finger.

After everything that I was doing, imagine my surprise when I'm sitting at his church anniversary waiting for him to be honest about what we had going on and finally let my best friend know that we were going to be together and in walks my beloved sister. The moment she let it be known that she was his other woman I knew that he had played me again. I could have died right there on the spot because I felt like as much as she hated me when she saw me she was going to blow my cover.

Once again she had come out on top and was catered to and someone chose her over me. I couldn't take it and I had no more fight left in me. I wanted to take the cowardly way out but even that didn't work.

I called her that night and told her I was going to kill myself and she had the nerve to ask me what took so long. The big sister that I needed was not there and I was finally tired.

Now here I was sitting in this nasty jail with women constantly calling me a 'baby killer'. I had heard stories about how they treated people in jail that hurt innocent children and I honestly prayed someone would take me out of my misery.

Looking up at the screen I saw a press conference beginning and a familiar face stood before the cameras. I knew this face so well because he was the reason I never knew that my sister was sleeping with Drew again. It was like once I told her I was pregnant with DJ she made it seem like she was over the whole thing and just wanted to move on with her life. She was still mad at me for getting pregnant by Drew but she had a new man in her life to make up for it. At least that was what she told me. Of course I couldn't tell Drew what was up because he didn't know we were related. I just relied on the fact that she was bowing out gracefully and I was about to be on top.

All of the promises he was making to me and DJ were what kept me holding on. He kept telling me how he couldn't wait until he could move on with me and be a real family. He was tired of faking the holy life as he called it and since he was already taking care of our every need I knew it would only be a matter of time.

But I began to get impatient over the years and was ready to move on. Drew was taking too long and I guess he thought I was playing when I told him that he had until his anniversary or I was going to expose us. Only I didn't get those honors.

Focusing back on the present the wheels in my head began to turning. I know I had no relationship with God like I was supposed and I could be wrong but I felt like He was telling me that this was my last chance to try and make things right. I just didn't know how to do it. That was until I tuned in to what was being said at this press conference.

"We are here live in front of the Mecklenburg County Sheriff's Department as the press conference into the disappearance of Kamiah Noel Webber. Police say that her father Pastor Andrew Webber was behind the kidnapping and that he and First Lady Jewel Webber were going through a messy divorce. There has been rumors that he was allegedly involved with another woman and together they were trying to extort money out of Jewel.

Let's tune in to what is being said." The reporter told the viewers.

It was like everyone around me were holding their breaths just like I was.

"Good afternoon. My name is Detective Jones and I am the lead investigator on this case. It is with a heavy heart that I inform the public that little Kamiah Webber has been found and she is deceased. Her body has been positively identified by her family.

This is a sad day for us all but it does not stop us from pursuing the culprit of the heinous crime. We are unsure if Mr. Webber was working alone or not. There is a fifteen million dollar reward for the arrest and conviction of Kammy's killer. At this time the cause of death and the information used to identify the body will remain confidential as this is still an open homicide investigation. That is all for now thank you."

Something didn't feel right about this as I thought about what I had just witnessed. I didn't know every detail about the case but I did know that this had Camilla written all over it as I watched the man I knew to be her husband leave the podium at this live press conference.

I knew that it would only be a matter of time before he found out I didn't die as planned and I was right here under his nose. I put nothing past Camilla so I knew that if I wanted to right my wrongs I had to move quick before it was too late.

Bryce

If someone would have told me years ago that this would be my life I would have called them crazy. Who would have thought that I would finally have a chance to be with the woman that my heart belonged to as well as the daughters her and I shared only for it all to be snatched away. It felt so unreal but riding in the back of the police car being accused of my daughter's death let me know that I wasn't dreaming.

When Detective Jones and the other officers walked into that church during my baby's funeral saying that they had a lead on a suspect, never in a million years did I think they would accuse me.

That was my baby girl and I would never hurt my girls or their mother.

Lord Jewel. In a way I'm glad that she had been restrained when she flipped out calling me Drew because if she hadn't then there is no telling where her mind would have gone with this new turn of events. I honestly don't think that even if she was in her right mind she would have believed what they were saying but she was so out of touch with reality who knew what she was capable of.

Pulling up to the back of the station I waited for the two officers to take me out of the car and process me. I wasn't about to resist arrest. Especially with all of the recent police killings of black men and women. The last thing I wanted was to be added to that list. I knew that each of those officers that were in the wrong would one day be judged. Be it on earth or on judgement day but they were going to be held accountable. God just had a funny way of doing things.

I was lost in my own thoughts when I noticed that only one of the officers got out of the car and headed inside. The one driving was still inside of the car looking at me through the rearview mirror. Before I could imagine what he was thinking he spoke.

“You don’t remember me do you?” He asked me.

I tried hard to remember where I knew him from because he did look familiar.

“Nah.” I said being short. I didn’t mean to sound rude but here I was being implicated on a murder I didn't commit and he wanted to play 'Guess Who'.

"Noland. Noland Rogers. I lived next door to you and your parents back in Philly before you moved down south." He said bringing everything back to my remembrance.

"Oh yeah! Man it's been a long time. I'm surprised that you remembered me." I told him.

Noland and I used to hang tough as youngsters until we moved. He was like my best friend. We were both a little on the quiet side but that was my dude. He always said he was going to be a police officer when he grew up and I see he stuck to that.

"You walked out your dream of becoming an officer I see." I said to him with a light smile.

Although I was glad for this little reunion I was still torn up by the state of what was going on around me.

"Yeah man. I wanted to be one of the good guys but it seems like there are quite a few that are making it hard on the good ones." He said looking out of the window at some of the passing officers.

"Well we just got to do what we know is right and pray that God will do the rest." I responded to him.

"Did you ever become that minister that you wanted to be?" Noland asked remembering my career choice as well.

"Sure did but I don't know how many will follow me as I follow Christ if I ever get out of this mess."

"Look let me tell you this before my partner comes back out." He said turning in his seat to look at me through the bullet proof partition that separated the front and back seats.

"Even though we haven't seen one another in years and people can change over time I don't think you did this. Our parents still talk on the regular and my mother speaks so highly of you and all of your accomplishments. It's because of hearing about what you do in ministry that made me give my life over to Christ for real. I don't know thinking about all of the times we played church and how serious you got came back to my memory." He said chuckling.

I remembered those days so well. It was like something took over me and when I came to I was drenched in sweat and the kids we were playing with were all crying or laid out somewhere.

"Man I don't know what would happen those days. The presence of God would be so strong even at such a young age. God definitely doesn't care about how old someone is in order to use them. I knew that's why I wanted to be a minister and lead God's people. But I've fallen so bad and I'm not sure if God is punishing me or what." I told him as I leaned my head back on the seat.

"Come on bruh. Wasn't it you that told me that day I stole that candy bar from Mr. Willie's store that we all have sinned and fallen short of the glory of God but that's why He sent His son to forgive us?"

We were some rambunctious little boys back then. Mr. Willie owned our neighborhood candy store and all of the kids would go in there and try to get over on him from time to time. I never wanted to participate so the day that Noland came to my house with his stolen candy I instantly encouraged him to take it back and apologize. I don't know what made me quote Romans 3:23 at that particular moment but as soon as I did Noland puffed up his chest and walked back in the direction of the store.

Later that evening when it was time to go to bed, my father came in and told me what Noland did. He got his butt torn up once Mr. Willie walked him home so he could tell his parents and in doing so he told them that I was the one that encouraged him to go back and make it right.

"You're right. I have to trust and believe that I have already been forgiven." I said to him.

"God is going to work this out in your favor." He said sounding real confident.

"You got more faith than I do right now." Day by day it felt like my faith was dwindling and I didn't know what to do or say at times but continue to blame myself.

"All we need is faith the size of a mustard seed and a little investigation skills." Noland replied piquing my interest. I guess the look on my face asked the question that my mouth didn't say.

"I know I shouldn't tell you this and if anyone finds out I can lose my job. I was sent undercover to investigate a few officers and detectives that were accused of being on the payroll of one of the biggest drug dealers this side of the Mississippi. While doing that I stumbled upon something concerning the lead detective on your daughter's case. I'm not sure what is going on with him or what he has to do with it just yet. And since I can't personally dig into it or have anyone here do it because they may alert him I'm having some of my father's connections do it for me.

When this warrant for your arrest came across Detective Jones' desk and I heard about it I immediately volunteered to bring you into custody. God works in mysterious ways and I now understand why He led me here. Just be easy and let me get as much information as I can in order to help you. Whatever you do don't speak to any of them. I'm going to get you an attorney. Stay prayerful and in God's face while here. Use this time to spend with Him as He continues to guide you.

Now let me get you in here before they start getting suspicious." Noland blew my min with this one or should I say God did. He never ceased to amaze me and just when I thought there was no way out of this just like Abraham, God had given me a ram in the bush.

Drew

I woke up feeling like I was in a bar fight of some sort. I knew that I shouldn't have had that many drinks the night before. Especially since it's been so long since I had a drink. Jewel never did like for me to drink because I would always start trouble. Laughing I thought about how much trouble I caused when I wasn't drinking too. They just didn't see it.

You will reap what you sow son.

Looking around the room I thought I was tripping but if I was honest with myself I already knew that my time would be winding down. God wasn't pleased with me but what my flesh wanted outweighed what it was I knew I should have been doing.

I already knew I wasn't bout nothing and I honestly didn't care. If I was going to bust hell wide open then I might as well live it up while I'm here cause I won't be seeing paradise once I left here anyway. See a lot of people would wonder what happened to me in life that made me this way and my answer to them would be I was just born.

My parents were loving and I came from a good home. No one ever abused me or anything of that nature. I just preferred to do me and if you got hurt in the process oh well. Suck it up and get over it.

There were times though that I kind of felt bad for the kids that were involved. Even if Avery didn't like me it wasn't her fault that her mother was loose and stepped out on her relationship. That's what gets me about these so called church folks. They always pointing a finger or throwing rocks then hiding their hands. She couldn't have repented for sleeping with Bryce and conceiving one child because she turned around and did it again. This time after we were married.

Yeah I had my women, plenty of women that she didn't know about and I slept with them on a regular. But Bryce was my boy and that should have been off limits. Now I know what you're thinking, Jasmine and Jewel were supposed to be best friends so how can the pot call the kettle black. Jasmine was only in it for self gain just like I was. When I found out that Bryce was digging

Jewel, I mean really digging her, I knew I had to step in quick if I had any chance of getting her to come up off of that money. I just didn't know I would have to waste all of those years and go through all of these hoops to get it.

Putting all of that to the back of my mind I finally made it out of the bed and into the bathroom to handle my morning procedure. Once I was done I felt a little better but I knew that I had to get something on my stomach and fast.

I called out to Kammy and she didn't answer me. Since the day I abducted her she hasn't said a word to me. The look she gave whenever Constance or I was around was amusing to me. If looks could kill we would definitely be dead. I had to admit though, how she was acting towards me wasn't something that I was used to. This kind of treatment was common coming from Avery but Kammy had always been my little princess no matter what. I guess she was tired of my mess too.

Walking into the kitchen I headed straight for the fridge to see what I could whip up real quick. It was close to noon so I knew breakfast was a no go. I pulled out the ingredients to make me a sandwich, got a cold Pepsi, and headed to the living room. Either Kammy was asleep or she was just ignoring me but I knew once that little stomach got to growling she would come around.

Enjoying my sandwich as I flipped through the channels I almost choked as I swallowed my drink. There on CNN was a broadcast that said the manhunt for Kamiah Webber's killer had ended.

Her body had been found and identified by her mother. Not only did that have me confused but to hear that Bryce was the one they had in custody threw me completely off.

This had to be some kind of joke because Kammy was just here when I went to sleep I thought as I ran into the room where she should have been. Upon opening the door I noticed that everything that belonged to her was gone. There was no trace of her even being here. I started to panic thinking that somehow she had gotten away and if that was the case then sooner or later someone would start digging and find us. The thing that confused me though was that the report said she was found not too far from her school. That was in North Carolina and we were currently in Tennessee. How was that possible when she was just here only hours before. Something just wasn't adding up.

Before I could process anything else I heard the keys being placed in the door and the lock becoming undone. Thinking it was Constance I ran towards the front room and came face to face with some woman I had ever seen before.

"I see you are finally awake huh?" she said walking over to place her purse on the end table.

Being that I had never seen her a day in my life before I didn't know why she looked so familiar to me. She stood about five foot four and had skin the color of butterscotch. Her face looked like she had gone through years of hell but you could tell that back in her day she was a stunner.

Whoever said back don't crack were not talking about her because her black had shattered years ago.

Her eyes held a lot of hurt and disappointment in them and her salt and pepper hair tried peeking out from under the lace front wig she sported. Now this woman had to at least be in her late fifties but her body was still banging. That face had seen better days but her body was on point I thought as I licked my lips.

She must have read my mind with what I was thinking because a sly smirk came across her face.

"In your dreams baby. You should have had enough of the women in my family." She said throwing me off. What did she mean by that?

"Who are you and what are you doing here?" I wanted to know. I watched her as she walked past where I was previously sitting eating and watching tv just a few minutes ago.

"Did I interrupt your meal?" she asked ignoring my question.

Walking back over to the couch I sat down and began to finish my food. Just that fast my mind had forgotten the situation with Kammy and was now focused on this woman.

"My name is Regina. I'm-" she began before I cut her off.

"Constance's mother." I finished for her.

"Indeed. So where's my cut?" Regina asked.

"What are you talking about?" The look on her face told me something was up but I didn't know what. One thing I did know was that this sandwich was starting not to agree with me.

"Don't play with me Drew. I know just as soon as that boy was arrested the money was deposited into an account for the person who called in the tip. I didn't do all of this just because I messed up back in the day. Well that was part of it but I want my money." She said standing up and walking over to where I was.

"I see why my daughters were so infatuated with you. Your daddy is probably fine just like you. Shoot had I gotten a hold to you I may have had your baby too!" Regina said falling out laughing.

Now I know I have never met Regina before and the only reason I knew her name was because

Constance had mentioned her a time or two. I also knew that she was the one who got the rental car for us the night I gave us away to Jewel. Never had I ever seen a picture of her but her eyes reminded me of Constance as well as someone else. Wait what did she mean by 'her daughters' being infatuated with me?

"You know I don't understand how after all of these years your wife and that flock you were supposed to be over couldn't see right through this façade. You wear your thoughts on your face. You are wondering what I meant when I said daughters huh?" This woman was dead on.

"Well yeah." It was starting to get hot in the room and I didn't know if it was because of how intensely she was staring me down or the ac needed to be turned down some but I was starting to sweat bullets.

Regina slid the plate and cup over to the side of the table and sat right in front of me. Had I not done so much wrong in my life I would have begun praying because something was terribly wrong. But I knew in my heart that God wouldn't intervene this time. He had given me many chances to come back to Him and I declined. I knew at this moment He was far from me like He never knew me.

"Calm your breathing down before you cause yourself to croak before I get to pour you all of this tea. It's only a little succinylcholine and I didn't give you that much to kill you anyway. You should really pay attention to where you sit your drinks, anyone could put something in it when you aren't looking."

Just then it hit me when she walked slowly in front of the table she must have dropped the potentially deadly muscle relaxant in my soda.

"Does the name Camilla Ropier ring a bell?" she asked me. It sounded familiar but I couldn't place it. And why was she asking me a question knowing that I couldn't open my mouth to speak.

"Oops you can't talk huh? My bad. Just think back to high school and the day when you were confronted about getting the 'mark' as you called her pregnant. Remember now?" she said with a sinister grin on her face.

Absolutely remembered now. That was a big bullet I dodged back then but what did that have to do with her?

"Well since you humiliated her and decided to have her beat within inches of losing her life she could no longer have children. She had to have a hysterectomy and that ended any chance of her becoming a mother. Not to mention her face was unrecognizable. My poor baby had to go through so many surgeries to reconstruct her face." Regina said as she cried.

I still wondered what Camilla had to do with why she was here. I haven't seen that girl since she handed me that sonogram in the cafeteria that day. When that girl came up to me my stomach dropped to the bottom of my feet and I knew that I had messed up. Never in a million years did I think something like that would happen.

The fellas had dared me to hook up with her and I even got some money out of the deal. What I didn't want was some kid by her. Had I cared I probably would have worked something out with her but I wasn't about to be a father to someone that I wanted no dealings with. I knew that if she had that baby I could kiss my future goodbye as I became another deadbeat baby daddy. If there was an award for Dead Beat Father of a Lifetime that would have been me cause I wasn't trying to hear that.

Instead of having her go through all of that I helped her get rid of it. After that I had never heard from her again and she didn't return to school. My face must have shown some type of confusion because she continued.

"I wonder how after all of these years you never managed to catch on to what was going on around you. That's just like a narcissist only thinking of themselves and to hell with how anyone else feels. You were so caught up that you didn't even take time to realize that Constance and Camilla are one in the same.

You see the last time you saw her she was just some little homely girl who hadn't come into her own just yet but once she had to have all of those surgeries her appearance was altered. Her body filled in in all of the right places, she kept her hair and wardrobe it and slid her way right back into your life. With the help of her sister of course." She confessed.

I couldn't believe what I was hearing right now. How in the world was this possible? It didn't sound real at all.

"What were the odds of you dealing with two sisters though? God must really have it out for you. I bet you wish you never played with Him huh? Down to the church trying to get people closer to God when you know good and well God don't even like yo' behind. All that lying and manipulating those people for your pleasure and thinking that you are God. Well baby if you are Him I would love to see how you get out of this here.

Did you really intend on marrying Jasmine like you said you were?" she asked me. How did she know about Jasmine?

"Dang I keep forgetting you slow. Jasmine is Camilla's baby sister. Oh hunty God got you so good. How do you church folks say it, He works in mysterious ways? Indeed He does. Too bad He didn't let His humble servant in on what was going on. Boy when I say I have some clever children. I may not care for Jasmine too much but she sure did play her part."

I didn't know if it was the medicine or if it was the information that I had received but I felt like I was needing to throw up at any moment.

How could I not see it all? Now that Regina had told me everything it was like my eyes were open and I couldn't believe that I had missed it all. Thinking back to the numerous times where I heard the Lord's voice telling me not to get involved with either of them I wish I had listened. I could have avoided a world of hurt had I just paid attention.

Constance, well Camilla, had indeed changed and had I looked closely I would have seen that it wasn't much. The first time I got her in bed her body felt so familiar to me. Like I had invaded her territory before. Now I knew that I had and this was going to cost me something that I wasn't willing to pay.

"So now that you are caught up where is the money? Camilla may be my child but I don't play about my coins." She said getting up walking around the house in search for her payout. I didn't know what she talking about because I had no money.

When Camilla told me not to worry about getting money for ransom because she had a better idea I asked her what it was she said that since I had messed up her plan from the beginning she wasn't telling me anything else until it was done. I was feeling just like the woman in the relationship being controlled by the man lately but I knew that if was because of what I had done. I tried making up for it but she didn't want to hear it.

The sound of a car door slamming and an alarm being activated I knew that it was Camilla. No one else knew where we were staying. Had I been able to move I probably would have choked her out as soon as she walked in the door after what her mother had just revealed to me. I couldn't believe that all of these years I had been fooled. Instead of me feeling remorse for what I had caused I felt nothing but anger. But wait, if she couldn't have children then where were the kids that she said we had together? The ones that I was doing all of this for in the first place so that we could be a family.

Immediately upon walking into the house Camilla walked right past me to the back of the house. The next thing I knew I was hearing nothing but yelling and what sounded like fighting between the two. I don't know what happened but just as quickly as it began it was over.

"I guess she told you everything huh?" Camilla asked me. She had come out of the room with what looked to be blood splatter on her clothes and I could only imagine what had happened.

"How could you?" I said finally able to get out a few words. I guess the medicine was wearing off.

"How could I? How could I Drew? My dude you did this to me! Because of you I lost our daughter and now I can't have kids! My husband deserves to have children by his wife." She fumed.

"Wait what?" I asked trying my best to sit up but was still unable to move like I needed to. Did this woman just tell me that she was married?

“That’s right I’m married and as soon as the reward money is posted into the account I will be on my way.” She said gathering some of her stuff.

“Where is Kammy? What did you do to her!” I yelled.

“So now you are the worried father. You want to protect her all of a sudden? Well it’s too late for the father of the year award. You messed that up when you murdered my baby. So I just returned the favor. What does the good book say? An eye for an eye right Pastor?” and with that she walked out of the house.

Avery

Being shocked would be an understatement when I received a call from jail the day before yesterday and it was my so called God mother Jasmine on the phone. I didn't have any words for her and was just about to hand up in her face until she said she had some information that could possibly help us. She didn't want to talk over the phone but she told me that visiting day was coming up and if I would come she would tell me everything.

I hesitated at first because I was so bitter towards her and how she hurt our family all of these years but I had to put it all behind me if I was going to get whatever information out of her so I agreed.

Here I was waiting on her to be brought out and getting even more impatient as the minutes dragged by. After about forty five minutes the door opened to the room and in she walked. I was used to seeing her look flawless but now she looked a mess. I could tell she was stressed out and quite frankly she had the right to be and in no way was she about to get any sympathy from me. She must have picked up on my vibe because that smile she had when the door opened was no longer present.

"Hey Ave." she said. This was not about to be a friendly meeting so all of the pleasantries were put on the back burner as I sat quietly mugging her.

"I know I'm the last person that you want to see but let me just say that I am truly sorry for what I did. If I could take it all back I would but I know that's impossible."

"Mmm hmmm." Was my only reply.

"Because of my selfish ways I lost my child so I can imagine the pain that Jewel is feeling."

"What do you mean you lost your child too?" I asked.

The waterworks started before she could answer and I felt nothing.

"I killed my baby. He didn't do a thing wrong but because of my greed and lust he's gone."

Did this looney woman just say she killed her son and she understands how my mother felt?

“There is no way that you can feel the pain my mother is feeling! You killed your baby and someone took Kammy from us. You made that choice we didn’t have one. How dare you compare the two?” I was trying my hardest not to yell because I didn’t want to draw any attention to us and possibly end this visit too soon.

“You are right this is all my fault and this is why I want to make it right. I knew that Jewel wouldn’t come talk to me that’s why I called you. I’m not sure if I’m a hundred percent accurate but here goes.”

I couldn’t believe what was told to me as I thought about everything Jasmine said. None of this sounded real. It had to be some cruel sick joke someone was playing with us.

Going straight home I went into my room and shut the door. I needed some alone time with God to make sure that what was told to me was true. It gave me a glimmer of hope and I just prayed that God would reveal all in due time.

"God I need you more than ever right now. Both of my parents are in a situation that only you can bring them out of. Do it like only you can." I said aloud as I dialed James' number.

Jewel

Sitting in my hospital bed I just stared at the wall. No amount of preparation could have me ready to face the things in life that I was at this very moment. The moment the police came in and arrested Bryce it was like everything stopped. There was absolutely no way that Bryce could be responsible for something like this. He loved our girls more than anything and would never hurt them. To me this had Drew and his female written all over it. I knew that I had to get myself together in order to find out what happened to my baby and make sure that everyone involved were held accountable.

There was a knock at the door before it was pushed open and Nia walked in. Nia was James' mother and she was also soon to be Avery's mother in law. For the last few days she has been coming to check on me. After my breakdown she took time off from work to come here and see about me. It was funny how God placed people in our lives for times that we never saw coming but they were there right when we needed them. Yesterday was the first day that I really held a conversation with anyone and that was when she helped me realize that if I wanted to get out of here and find out what was really going on then I had to come out of that funk that I was in. No one would take anything I said seriously if I was in here drugged up and talking out of my head.

She helped me to see that it was nothing but the enemy that wanted me to stay bound like that because if I was in my right frame of mind he knew that I would uncover his mess. I was determined to get out of here and I needed to get out soon. Right now Bryce needed me in order to get out of jail and just like he had always been there for me I was going to be there for him.

"How are you feeling J?" Nia asked me walking over to me and giving me a tight hug. You couldn't tell at all that she had had children not too long ago because her body bounce back like it was nothing.

"I'm better. I thought about what you said and I know I have to get a clear mind if I want to get out of here. Kammy may not be here but I still have to be here for Ave and find out the real killer because Bryce isn't the one."

"I know he didn't do it either. The first time we met him I knew that he was a true man of God. He would never do such a thing." She said pulling a chair up beside the bed.

"Nia when they showed me the pictures of the crime scene and my baby's body I swear I thought that was the end of me at first. But then something didn't feel right."

"What do you mean?"

"I don't know but looking at that picture caused so many emotions to run through me. The main one being that wasn't my baby."

"I know you want to believe that's not Kammy but she was positively identified honey.

Never does a parent want to have to deal with the loss of a child. When I was first told that I had lost one of the twins I was so depressed. I didn't want to believe it." She told me.

"You knew in your heart he was still alive in your womb didn't you?" I asked her.

"Yeah. I did." She sighed.

"And he was. You knew it because mothers know when our kids are hurting and I feel like my sweet little girl is in so much pain." I broke out crying as Nia go up and sat beside me on the bed gently rocking me.

Neither of us said a word to one another for at least fifteen minutes. She just let me cry and get it all out. I was in desperate need of prayer and without me asking she began praying in her heavenly language. After a few moments I couldn't help but to join in as we let the Holy Spirit have His way in here. With each utterance I could feel myself getting stronger again and I knew that this fight was going to be won and the devil once again would be defeated.

By the time we were done praying I had gotten up out of the bed and was walking around praising God. A couple of times one of the nurses came to check in on us to make sure we were ok. I could tell she didn't understand what we were doing but we kept right on going.

"My God the anointing in this room." I heard come from behind me.

Turning around I saw an older gentleman walk in carrying some files in his hands. He looked exactly like an older version of Nia's husband Jerrod so I knew they had to be related in some kind of way.

"Jewel this is my father in law Rob. He is a retired detective and there are some things that he wanted to come and talk to you about. That's the main reason I came but when I got here you were in no condition to talk right away. I took a chance with bringing him here today praying that you were in a better mindset." She said introducing us.

"I hate that we are meeting under such circumstances but I know that it is not by coincidence." He started out.

My parents had always taught us that nothing that happens is out of coincidence but all a part of God's perfect design. Our steps are already ordered by Him and it's only a matter of time before we begin to realize it.

"It's nice to meet you." I told him reaching out to shake his hand.

"I won't be long because I know that you need your rest." He said pulling up the other chair and moving the dinner tray closer to where he was. I walked back over to the bed with Nia sitting down beside me.

"Between my grandson talking to me about what was going on, the news reporting everything, and speaking to a family friend I've uncovered something major. This could possibly exonerate Bryce as well as tell us what really happened to Kammy and the person or persons behind it."

For the first time since all of this started I started to feel hopeful just by hearing that little bit of information.

"When James came to me and asked if I could look into the case for him I told him I would. Being that I was in Georgia and this happened here I didn't know how I could get what I needed without drawing attention to myself. But see when God is in it He will give you everything that you need to accomplish the task set before you." Rob told us while opening the folder that he had on the table and looking through the contents of it.

"You won't get in any trouble by doing this will you Dad?" Nia asked him concerned.

"If I do but the information pans out in our favor then it will all be worth it. Now what I say today stays between us until it's all verified. Got it?"

Both Nia and I nodded our heads and I prayed that he would hurry up and tell us what he had. He must have sensed me getting impatient because he continued.

"One of my college buddies reached out to me the same day that James and I talked. I felt like that couldn't have been better timing. He said that his son was here working on an unrelated case but stumbled upon something that he couldn't look into himself without blowing his cover.

Does the name Detective Nasir Jones ring a bell?" he asked me.

"That's the lead detective on Kammy's case." I told him.

"Well it looks like Detective Jones isn't who he really says he is. Nasir is married to a young woman by the name of Camilla Ropier-Jones."

"Who? I don't know anyone by that name and what does that have to do with anything?" I wondered.

"Camilla is also known as Constance." He said like I should immediately know. The name was vaguely familiar and then it hit me.

"OH MY GOD! That's the woman that came in the church saying she was the pastor's other woman and Drew left with her!" This was all too much and nothing was making sense.

"Bingo! He and Camilla have been married for the last fifteen years. She is originally from here but moved to Tennessee when she was just eighteen. She moved because of Drew."

"Wait a minute. So you mean to tell me they have been messing around since high school?" I asked.

"Yes and no. Upon further digging I found out that Camilla had gotten pregnant by Drew their senior year of high school but he was the cause of them losing their daughter. He had her beaten so badly that she had to have surgeries to repair her face and a hysterectomy causing her to not be able to have kids.

When Drew saw her again he had no idea she was the same person and he also didn't know that he was sleeping with her younger sister

Jasmine either." Rob just dropped a bomb on me so big North Korea would be jealous.

"Jasmine as in Jasmine Jasmine. The one I went to school with Jasmine. The one who is the Godmother of my daughters Jasmine." Shocked would not begin to describe what I was feeling right now. This was unbelievable and if I wasn't here listening to Rob and seeing all of the evidence he was pulling out I still may not have believed him.

"The very same one." He told me.

I looked as he passed me not only pictures of Constance when she was known as Camilla but he had found documents backing up everything. Come to find out that Camilla was the one that came up with the whole idea of getting back at

Drew for what happened to her baby. When Jasmine learned from me about the money I had coming in she wanted it all to herself. Not only did Drew play me but he played her too by making her think they were going to be a happy family.

Drew had hurt the both of them in so many ways but I had no sympathy towards either of them. That still didn't explain why Jasmine betrayed me so I asked.

"Well she told Avery when-." he started.

"Hold on when did my daughter talk to Jasmine?" Tea was pouring like the land that overflowed with milk and honey and I couldn't catch it all.

"From my understanding Jasmine reached out to Avery saying she wanted to make everything better and help you get closure. Since she is locked up now she wanted to come clean."

"Locked up? For what?" Where was all of this coming from? The last time I saw Jasmine she was fighting Drew and who I now know to be her sister in the church office.

"Apparently the day everything went down at the church Jasmine returned to her hotel room and tried to commit murder suicide by killing her son then herself. She was successful with the first part but she was saved before she died."

"How could a mother do that to an innocent baby?" This was too much to handle but I needed to know it all.

He told me about the conversation that Avery and Jasmine had and how he is confident that Detective Jones has his hands in this. He is originally from Tennessee and thinks that may be where Constance ad Drew took Kammy. If so because they crossed state lines this would now be looked into by the FBI. I was worried that they would be tipped off but he comforted me by letting me know that with the nature of the crime and him being law enforcement they would do all they could for him not to be let on.

We were to still talk to him as normal if he dropped by and not give him any indication that we were on to him helping them. I have no clue how the main dude would be helping the side dude in a situation like this but I guess money made you do some weird things.

Rob let me know that he had found out where she worked thanks to what Jasmine told Avery so he was going to try and get in touch with her employer and coworkers to see if they could possibly help him tie everything together. It might take a few days but he was going to move as fast as he could now that he had the information and backup that he needed.

As hopeful as all of that sounded I still couldn't celebrate because my little girl would still be dead even after everything had come to the light. But I did find a little comfort in knowing that all involved would be brought to justice and Bryce would be set free.

Bryce

"People of God don't even read their Bibles There's no faith no trust in the word...But everybody seems to be quoting scripture... It's just another word they heard Pastors leaving pulpits cause they're tired It's all based on how we feel Overheard two people speaking the other day One said that God's not real but...I'm just one ah them ole people who's got to hold on. Sometimes I can't see but I still believe He's taking care of me...Oh oh oh I'm just one ah them ole people God's got a hold on And I believe, I believe, ... Yeah! I believe I believe... Yeah!" I sang as my cellmate came back inside to his bunk. If Mali Music didn't hit the nail on the head with that song I don't know who did.

It made me think about the times we were faced with and how so many people seem to be blind to the times. I know that I have made my fair share of mistakes but that didn't mean that I stopped believing in God. No matter what it looked like or how I felt I would always trust Him.

"Why?" asked my cellmate. For a minute I thought maybe I had been talking out loud instead of thinking the thoughts that had just crossed my mind.

"Why what?" I asked sitting up.

I looked at the young white gentleman sitting across from me. He looked to be no older than twenty. The weary expression he wore let me know that he had had a rough life so far and was about to give up on life. His sandy brown hair was unkempt and his icy blue eyes looked weary. The tattoos that he wore told a story of pain mixed with hope. Always being a reminder of where he had come from and what he had done. He was so close to giving up and it wouldn't take much to get him to that place.

"Never mind man. Forget it." He said. I knew he wanted to talk but he was unsure of the unknown.

"I believe in God because without Him I would have been dead and gone long ago." I told him honestly. Some of the things I witnessed when I was growing up would have surely sent me to an early grave had it not been for God.

"Do you believe?" I asked him. Turning back to face me he just stared at me a moment before responding.

"Nah."

"Do you mind me asking why not?"

"If God was here for me He wouldn't allow my life to be the way that it is. Why won't He make it right?"

I could see all of the years of hurt and pain he was dealing with as it poured from his eyes and ran down his face.

"Have you allowed Him to?" I asked him. I knew he was confused so I continued.

"Out of all of the things that you have gone through have you taken the time to go to Him and lay it all at His feet?"

"Why do I have to do that? He's God and supposed to be able to do anything right?" Anger was starting to set in and I knew that if I wanted to be a witness to this young man I had to hurry before he shut down.

"God is a gentleman and He doesn't force Himself on any of us. He wants us to come to Him and let Him in our lives on our own free will. But we first have to accept Jesus into our lives and repent of our sins."

"How do I do that?"

"Simply confess that He is the son of God, He died and rose again so that we might be free from the punishment of all sins. Then we have to repent of all of those sins."

"That's it? I don't have to do any chanting or nothing?" He asked and I laughed.

It amazed me when people thought that God was so difficult and that they had to do more than what is required to be saved. Maybe that's why it was so many people not willing to do it because it sounded too simple to them.

"No chanting required. Only an open and willing heart to let Him in and be your savior." I was praying that I was able to reach this young man for the kingdom but he was still looking unsure.

"What brought you in?" I asked changing the subject for a minute.

"Armed robbery. Me and my homeboy ran up in a house but I was the only one to make it out.

The homeowner wasn't trying to let up off of what we came for and next thing I know he was letting them thangs fly. Tone took two hot ones and died on the spot. I caught a bullet in the leg but I made it out. The next day twelve caught me at my baby mama's house sleep." He said shaking his head.

"How old is your child?"

"My little girl not even out the oven yet. She still baking." He said with a smile on his face. I could tell with just the thought of his unborn baby that she was his only hope.

"Do you want her to grow up without her father?"

"Of course not. The only reason I did what I did was for her in the first place. We needed the money." I knew that wasn't a good excuse but I understood how he was feeling. To him and his circumstance the reason was a valid one.

“Who do you think allowed you to make it out?” I asked him. I wanted him to think of the situation surrounding where he is now and come to the realization all on his own.

“God?” he asked like he was unsure.

“The one and only. See a lot of times we don’t look at the purpose of what we are going through because the pain is too great. It distracts us from what God is really trying to get us to see. You could have had the same fate that your friend did and not have another chance to get things right. So many people never get to make it right but He is giving you another chance. Not just for you but for your child.

I don't know if anyone has ever told you this but I see the hand of God on your life and this is only a pit stop to your destiny. But you have to want it." I revealed to him.

Looking past his circumstances and his appearance right now I see what God is doing in his life and I pray that he can tap into that. As much as I see in him and want him to make that step he has to want it for himself. You can definitely lead a horse to water but you couldn't make him drink if he wasn't thirsty. We have to be thirsty for Christ in order to get to where He wants us to be.

"I hear what you saying." Was all he said as he laid down on his bunk and wiped his face.

I didn't want to push so I let it be. I smiled to myself because the same thing that I had just told to Anthony about seeing the purpose in the pain God was now showing that to me. This young man was the reason I needed to be here at this very moment. I said a quick prayer silently and closed my eyes before the much needed sleep took over.

Samantha

I had twenty minutes to get to work before I knew a write up would be coming my way. Over the last couple of weeks I had been either late or out altogether trying to look out for Constance. That was my girl though and because I knew the situation with her mother I wanted to lift that burden as much as I could.

When I asked my aunt to help me care for her little sister she told me that she wouldn't be able to because she had so much work she needed to get caught up on. Going back on my word was not something that I did so I offered my assistance instead. I just couldn't get over the feeling that something was terribly wrong though.

The first few days were ok. The cute little girl Jasmine was no trouble at all but she didn't talk much. I had to force her to eat because I didn't want her getting sick on my watch. I figured she was just taking it hard knowing what was going on with her mother. Any child would have a hard time trying to cope especially at such a young age. Being removed from your home only to be placed with a stranger. I did my best though to make her feel at ease though.

Then a few days ago Constance called me telling me that she needed me to meet her downtown and bring her sister to her she was going back home. I was so happy when she told me that her mother made a turn for the better. I praised God for all that He has done for them. But all of that joy vanished when I watched as Constance grabbed little Jasmine out of my car. As long as I lived I would never forget the fear that was etched on her face. Constance didn't say anything as she drove off.

Throwing caution to the wind I took it as she was just in a hurry and because I didn't tell Jasmine her mother was better she may have thought something bad had happened to her.

I knew that I probably should have just called my aunt so I wouldn't be late but here I was driving over to my aunt's house to let her know the good news. I knocked on the door. Immediately she came to the door in a panic.

"Aunt Rosa what's the matter?" I asked concerned.

“Where is Jasmine?” she said ignoring my question and opening her screen door to allow me access to her home.

“I dropped her off to Constance a few days ago. Her mother is better now so I came to tell you before I headed in to work. I’m about to be late but what’s wrong?”

“Baby when I told you I couldn’t watch her it wasn’t really because I was busy. I had a gut feeling that something fishy was going on but I wasn’t sure. I knew she would be good in your care so I wasn’t worried.

Anyway I have been praying and praying that God let me know what was going on and what I needed to do but when I didn’t get an answer I tried to let it go until a few moments ago. I was just about to call you but I saw you pulling up. I was hoping to see Jasmine with you but my God this can't be good." She said scaring me and walking over to the television in her den.

Picking up the remote control she began to rewind the news she was watching and that's when I saw Jasmine's picture on the screen with the word "DECEASED" under her photo. I covered my mouth to keep from yelling as I listened to the news coverage. To hear that the little girl I had come to know as Jasmine was really an abducted child named Kamiah Webber made me sick.

The news that her body had been found took me to my knees. Why hadn't I known something was wrong? That's why she was so quiet. All this time I'm thinking that she was worried and missing her sick mother and in actuality she was being held against her will and I was helping.

God knows if I had known what was really going on I would have never gotten involved. I needed to make this right now that I knew what was going on. I had no idea that Constance could be capable of anything like this and I was usually a good judge of character. My spirit of discernment must have been turned off because she got right past me. I really considered her my friend.

Before I could get to the phone to call the police there was a knock at the door. Aunt Rosa and I stood frozen in place when we heard someone on the other end saying they were a detective. I ran over to the door and came face to face with an older gentlemen. He showed me his badge and I let him inside.

"Good morning my name is Detective Rob Stevenson and I'm looking for a Ms. Samantha Harper." He said.

"I'm Samantha. Please in." I said opening the door wider allowing him access. "This is my Aunt Rosa."

"It's a pleasure." They both said shaking hands.

"I know you are probably wondering why I'm here and how I knew where to find you." He said reading my mind.

"I think I know why you are here but it is surprising that you aren't at my house."

“Initially I went by your job first looking for someone else. When they told me she hadn’t been to work in a few days your boss suggested that I come and speak with you. Out of everyone there I was told that you two were the closest. I got to you apartment just as you were rushing out. I thought maybe you had been tipped off so instead of causing a scene I followed you here. I was hoping that you were leading me to who I was in search of.

Are you familiar with a young woman by the name of Camilla Ropier-Jones?” he wanted to know.

The name didn’t ring any bells and I looked over at my aunt who shrugged her shoulders indicating that she didn’t either.

"Maybe you know her by Constance?"

My eyes got as big as saucers when he mentioned her name.

"Oh Lord yes! I was just about to call the police before you came." I replied.

"Why is that?" he asked pulling out a notebook.

I filled him in on everything I knew about Constance all the way up until I dropped Kamiah off to her a few days ago. By the time I finished my story I was crying again because I felt bad turning her back over to that woman. It felt like I was the cause of her death.

Detective Stevenson explained to me everything that he knew so far and needed my help in order to find her. I was willing to do anything that I could. It hurt to know that I couldn't help bring her back alive but I would do anything that I could to put everyone responsible behind bars.

I thought long and hard about anything that I could tell him to lead him to Constance but was drawing up a blank. That was until I remembered where she lived. I didn't know the exact address but on one of the weekends that we hung out she had gotten so drunk that she couldn't drive home. I had one of my other friends drive my car as I drove Constance home. I remembered the area and would know the house if I saw it but the exact address was unknown.

Having this new piece of information he pulled out his phone and stepped away to place the call.

“I can’t believe this is happening.” I said to my aunt as she walked up to me and put her arms around me.

“Baby it’s not your fault what happened to that little angel. Had you knows sooner I know you would have protected her. I had a feeling something wasn’t right and I kept praying for a revelation. Lord knows I just hate this was the end result.” She said trying her best to comfort me.

Walking back into the room Detective Stevenson asked me if I would show him the house. I agreed as my aunt threw on her shoes and grabbed her purse. It would have been comical under different circumstances how fast she was moving around so she wouldn’t get left behind.

Locking up we got into the detective's car as I silently prayed God would intervene.

Drew

This was not the way that our plan was supposed turn out and I finally realized that this was payback for the many years I have lived this lie and the many people that I hurt in the process. To hear that Kammy had died did something to me. God knows I never intended for her to get hurt in such a way but the greed for the money and the lust of women sealed her fate.

If I could take it all back I would. It should never had gotten to the lace of something so bad happening for me to open my eyes but it did and now I was suffering the consequences of my decisions.

Nothing could have prepared me for what Camilla's mother told me. I thought back on that time and I remembered that was the first time I had heard God's voice giving me a warning. He told me not to mess with that girl and even after she told me she was pregnant He encouraged me to make it right. I just couldn't. My pride meant more to me than anything and I was nowhere near ready to have a child. Especially by someone of her caliber.

Camilla was not attractive to me at all. She didn't fit the bill at all for what I wanted on my arm. I was the man in school and my boys would have blasted me had I tried to get serious with her and be a father to her baby. It was already bad enough I had to sleep with her as a dare.

Bryce even tried warning me about not doing anything stupid. No one knew what I had planned when I got a few of the girls I was rocking with to jump on her. I even sat in the cut and watched them do it. When she didn't come back to school and no one ever saw her again I was relieved and went on my merry way. I guess that statement about *hell hath no fury like a woman scorned* was nothing but the truth.

Not only had I scorned Camilla but Jewel, Jasmine, Avery, and Kammy had felt it in one way or another. I thought about the family I once had. Any man would have been blessed to have them in his life and I took advantage of it all. Instead of letting Bryce get with Jewel I stepped in first.

I will never forget the day that he told me he was feeling her. It was right after Jasmine had put me up on game about her money and all I saw was dollar signs. When he told me he was checking for her I immediately told Jasmine to put a bug in her ear about us hooking up. That night I saw her at the party I made the first move but I made it seem like it was all her in front of Bryce. That way he couldn't be mad at me for stepping to her. There was no way I was letting her out of my site with that much money involved.

So many people say that money is the root of all evil but that not what the word of God says. It clearly says that for the *love* of money is the root of all evil. I loved money more than I loved anything else and having a bad chick on my arm was just a plus.

When I saw Constance for the first time at a church service and I saw how she was eying me once again I was warned. And once again I didn't take heed to the warning. I can't even say that if I could go back I would have done anything different cause honestly I wouldn't. Now I may not have been one of the most honest to others but to myself I was. I knew I was wring and I knew that what I was doing was to solely benefit me and there would have been nothing I would have changed then. But bringing Kammy into the picture, that would be something that I wished I could go back and change. I can only imagine the fear she felt and the man who was supposed to protect her had let her down in the worst way.

I had no idea how Jewel and Avery were coping but I had hoped Jewel didn't take her own life behind me and my selfish ways. I really couldn't live with myself if knowing that I was the root cause of it all. Jewel was a good woman and deserved someone to really love and protect her heart. I had messed that up and I could now admit it.

Here I was trapped in this house with no way out. Once I got control of my muscles back I immediately went to go check on Regina. For the first time I was fearful of the unknown. When I opened that door and saw her lifeless body on that floor surrounded by blood I emptied the contents of my stomach until I was dry heaving. I was so focused on what we needed to do next that I didn't notice all of the windows and doors had those bars on them until I tried getting out.

Panic almost set in until I thought about just waiting until Camilla came back and I would over power her and get out. She was only able to leave the day before because I was unable to move but I noticed she didn't say she wouldn't be returning. I had come up with the perfect plan to deal with her when she got back and all I had to do was wait. That was until I saw the flashing of blue lights from the living room window.

I had to come up with something because when I peeked out of the curtains I knew I was surrounded but how did they find me? Camilla had to have told them where I was but why would she do that and rick getting caught too. Just as I thought of the most feasible explanation that I could come up with the front door came crashing down and the thought of a dead woman being in the other room.

It was over for me I thought as the officers yelled at me to get down on the ground and I obliged. Just like the enemy knew the word of God because he was once an angel of light so did I. At this very moment the scripture that came to the forefront of my mind was Revelations 20:10

"And the devil who deceived them was thrown into the lake of fire and brimstone, where the beast and the false prophet are also; and they will be tormented day and night forever and ever."

Being honest with myself as the officers read me my rights and escorted me to an awaiting patrol car, I understood that my torment had begun long ago and it was nowhere near over.

Constance

"I tried telling you that Regina should have been dealt with a long time ago. She was only out for self when she knew how much money we were getting." Nasir said.

I hated to agree with him but he was right. I should have never told her how much money we were getting because up until then she was cool playing her role. It was a trip how money changed people.

"Yeah you right but we don't have to worry about her now. This time tomorrow we will be well on our way to our new lives." I told him rubbing his handsome face.

Detective Nasir Jones was the finest man I had ever seen. I met him shortly after we moved to Tennessee. When I met him I was at my worst and he accepted that. I was even honest about why I ended up where I was. Nasir was there through the beginning stages of my reconstructive surgeries so he knew the old and new me and he fell in love just the same. He was the first man that really showed me that they loved me for who I was.

The day that I told him how I had grown to hate Drew so much because he was the reason no man would ever want me, he didn't hesitate to take me down to the courthouse and prove to me how much he really loved me. Instead of hightailing it out of there I welcomed him with opened arms and we started our lives together.

He was just about to go off to the police academy because he had always desired to become a detective and because he was there for me I supported him and his dream. While he was gone off to training that was when I went back home for a visit. Something in me was leading me to my sister. I felt bad on how she was treated and honestly didn't know if she was going to want anything to do with me but as soon as I saw her it was like none of that even mattered.

I had kept tabs on Drew and knew that once he graduated he went to Georgia for school. I had made a promise to myself that before God called me home or I bust hell wide open I was going to make him pay for all of the pain he caused me. There must have been someone praying for me cause when Jasmine told me that she had gotten accepted into Spelman I knew this was my time. What I didn't expect was for her to end up falling for Drew herself and coming up with her own plan.

When Nasir came back home and I filled him in on everything I just knew he was going to be against me but surprisingly he helped me come up with the best idea ever. For years we put things in motion and I had even convinced my sister that I was over Drew. I introduced her to Nasir and everything so that she would believe that I was done. She always had been one of the dullest crayons in the crayon box.

I was still messing with Drew and I knew that he wasn't going to tell anyone so Jasmine was the least of my concern. Nasir was a real man because he wasn't even bothered by me sleeping with someone else. He would always tell me he didn't mind sharing for the greater cause which was all of that money we would get in the end.

Some days I wanted to quit though because to me it shouldn't take that long to get that money out of old girl but Nasir had enough patience for the both of us. To this day I still don't know how Jewel found out what Drew was up to in order to change that deposit information. I honestly thing that Bryce had something to do with it. I tried telling Drew not to trust him but nooooo that was his boy and they were riding til the wheels fell off. I guess they sitting on cinder blocks now cause them wheels are long gone.

All in all it worked out in my favor as a wide smile spread across my face seeing the notification that a deposit had just hit my account. Nasir told me how those things worked with reward money and since he was able to plant all of the evidence needed to implicate Bryce it was an open and shut case for the DA.

"We did it baby!" I squealed as I turned the phone around so that he could see the amount.

"That's what I'm talking about!" he said getting hype.

We thought that maybe we would have to lay low tonight once we got to Miami but it looked like we would be able to leave as soon as we got in. I had changed my hair color and style, threw some colored contacts in, an even changed how I dressed so I couldn't be identified. The good thing about being married to an officer of the law was that he knew criminals that could get us fake documentation for anything we needed. As soon as we got off of the road we were going to board a ship to the islands. From there we would catch a flight to anywhere in the world that we wanted leaving this life behind for good.

Who said blessings only came from God? Hmph the devil knows how to take care of his own too and my bank account with all of those zeros proved it!

Bryce

Service had just ended and tonight we had four more inmates give their lives over to Christ. After talking to Anthony that night one of the guards told me the next morning that the warden wanted to speak with me. Once I was escorted down to his office he asked me if I would mind doing some Bible study a few night a week. He had heard I was a minister and had been following the care so he knew all about me. He wished that he could let me go because he just didn't think I was responsible for any of what I was being charged with.

I agreed since I had nothing else to do and if I was going to preach to Anthony about still trusting God while I'm going through the trials I had to show him as well. The first night there were only about six of us total an Anthony decided that he was ready to make that step and turn his life around. The next day his lawyer met with him to let him know that he would be getting out sooner than he thought if the information he received panned out. All I could do was praise God for him and encourage him to be the best man that he could be when he got out. Not just for his daughter but for himself too.

This last service was a powerful one and around thirty men attended. Some were still skeptical and wanted to go back and forth with what they called scientific proof that God didn't exist. I let them get those thoughts off of their chest before I continued my teachings and at the end of the time we shared together more were wanting to be closer to God.

I gathered all of my notes and bible as I headed out of the back of the room towards Warden Green. He had been standing there for the last thirty minutes with a look that I could read.

"Hey there Pastor." He greeted me.

"How you doing Warden? You here later than usual tonight." I observed. Usually when five hit he was out of the door headed home to his family and here it was almost seven in the evening and he was still here.

"Yea but it's for a good cause. Follow me to my office real quick." He said and started walking down the corridor. He wasted no time getting right to business.

"Would you mind continuing a prison ministry here a few nights a month?" he asked me.

I was confused because I already told him I would and have been doing that. If I couldn't be out there free spreading the gospel I would going to do it right here and no devil in hell could stop me.

"I already told you that I would. Mistry is what I love to do." I told him.

"Yes I know you said you would while you were here but I want to know will you continue once you leave?" he said with a hit of a smile in his eyes. What was he saying? I had just been found guilty without a trial because the evidence pointed to me and my attorney had yet to get an appeal.

"What are you talking about? I'm confused."

"You go home in the morning." This time he couldn't hide the smile.

"Huh? What? How? Wait what's going on?" I was so confused but filled with so much joy at the same time.

"You lawyer called me a little while ago and let me know that you would be getting out first thing in the morning. He asked that I let him tell you the specifics."

Before I realized it I was crying and speaking in tongues. Once again my God had come through on a wing and a prayer making a way out of no way. No one could tell me that the God I serve did not take care of his people!

When I got back to my cell I told Anthony the good news and he celebrated with me. He wanted to know that once he got out if he could keep in contact with me. Now that he had changed his life for the better he wanted to stay on the right path and have me mentor him. He said no one ever cared enough to talk to him like he did and he even encouraged his baby mama to accept Jesus into her heart and her life.

That night I went to sleep for the first time in weeks with so much peace and joy in my heart that I'm sure the smile that I had never left my face.

Jewel

"Mommy stop shaking." Avery said as she sat beside me and put her hand on my thigh. I hadn't see her smile this much in what seemed like forever. She was starting to look like my baby again.

We were sitting inside of the waiting room of the jail with Bryce's lawyer, his officer friend that he grew up with, Nia, James, Jerrod, and Rob. It was like time was moving at a snail's pace once again as we waited for them to release Bryce.

I tossed and turned so much last night from excitement that I didn't fall asleep until the wee hours of the morning and was right up on time ready to get downtown. I couldn't catch the tears fast enough as they fell from my eyes.

We all heard the door buzz and turned in the direction. Standing there was Bryce as he looked like he was about to pass out at any moment from the sight before him.

"DADDY! DADDY!" Kammy screamed running full speed ahead. You could have knocked him over with a feather at that very moment. I knew he had so many questions that we would all fill him in on once he had this time with his baby girl. To hear the emotion in his cries made everyone in the room break down as well.

Bryce kept pulling her back from him so that he could look at her and then seconds later he pulled her close to him again. I watched as he touched her hair and her arms and I knew what he was doing. He was trying to make sure that she was real and he wasn't dreaming.

When Rob called us and said he was on his way to the house I was just expecting him to have information about finding Drew and Camilla. I had no idea the blessing that he was bringing to us.

With the help of Samantha, a woman that worked with Camilla, they were able to locate the house that she knew Camilla to live in. Drew was found inside along with Camilla's deceased mother. Instead of putting up a fight and resisting he let them take him. The only thing he had to say was that he was sorry and that he wanted me to know.

Jasmine was the one who helped piece everything together in order to track down Detective Jones and her sister. They were able to find out that he had family in Miami and more than likely they were headed that way in order to leave undetected. But the smart detective forgot that his police issued cell phone had a tracking device on it. With the help of the state patrol in Georgia they were able to set up a road block right before they crossed over into Florida.

They guessed that Nasir and Camilla knew they were caught but neither of them wanted to go to jail. The officers watched as the two of them sat in the car talking to one another before the backdoor on the driver's side opened slowly and

Kammy came running and crying into one of the officer's arms.

Before they could make sure Kammy was ok, Camilla had her husband try and flee but were stopped once again when the officers opened fire on the car they were in killing them on the scene.

I held on to Bryce for dear life because I never wanted to let him go. Because of the false pretenses Drew married me under and everything that had happened we were able to get a judge to have our marriage annulled. After twenty years together they were able to make it all go away.

***

Sunday morning rolled around and it was time to lay it all before the people. I knew that if we wanted to move forward in our lives there were some things that we had to ask forgiveness for. There was no way that we could continue to try and lead the people of God the right way if we weren't open about it all. Since I was the leader of this church I took it upon myself to let them all know about everything. I told them about the infidelities on all sides and I let them know that if they wanted to leave that we understood. But in no way would I stop us from ministering to those in need.

A few people decided this wasn't the church they wanted to be a part of any longer because church folks don't act like this. I was a little disappointed but I understood. Everything we had gone through was definitely a lot to deal with especially in the house of God. The last thing we wanted to do was embarrass God, our parents, or our congregation. We had done enough of that already.

Bryce took to the podium and I noticed someone in the front had caught his attention. Looking over in that direction I saw a young white couple sitting there and the woman looked to be ready to have that baby if she sneezed too hard. I knew who it was without him having to say anything because that's all Bryce talked about and I was glad that he had kept his promise to be there for him.

Reaching for my hand Bryce turned to me with the mic in his other hand.

"I know this may be sudden but the last time I waited too long to tell you how I felt it cost me years of heartache. I'm not saying the way we handled everything was right but I do feel that God has forgiven us. We have two beautiful daughters who deserve to see their mother happy and be loved the way she should. They should know that the man they marry should love them even more than I do." He said as he looked over at James and gave him the eye. James couldn't help but to laugh as he simply nodded his head in understanding and placed Avery's hand in his.

Turning back to me he continued, "I know that it will take some time for us to get back on track but I don't want to do it without you." He said before getting down on one knee and pulling out a ring box.

It was the ring that was passed down in his family to each daughter that got married. Since he didn't have a sister and Bryce's parents knew how much he loved me they wanted me to have it. The held on to it all of these years because they knew that one day I would be wearing it.

"Jewel Evette Rivers will you do me the honors of being this Pastor's *only* woman?" Bryce asked as he slipped the ring on my finger.

Yall know I said yes right?!

The End

Here's a little excerpt from the highly anticipated spinoff to 'Thuggin at the Altar' by Jenica Johnson and myself!

NO MORE THUGGIN

Chasiti

I was huge! Being a big girl already God knew I didn't need to gain any more weight but the way this pregnancy was set up I was miserable. My feet were constantly swollen, my nose looked big as ever, and I didn't even want my own husband touching me. Not that he wanted to anyway.

He had been real distant lately and I didn't know if it was because of me, the ministry he was now in charge of, or something else. Gavon never came home after 7pm which I appreciated but when he got there he was so tired and snappy. Most times he would eat the dinner I prepared, play a little with our daughter Jasmine, find out how my day went and then it was lights out by ten.

Once Mama Jean passed it just felt like he had taken on the weight of the world and I understood where he was coming from. It was like when she was alive she made life seem so much easier. Though she wasn't there in the natural we constantly felt her spirit daily and that gave me some comfort. Especially during this high risk pregnancy.

Gavon, Jr was a handful already and he wasn't even here yet. I can only imagine how he would be once he entered this world and in a few short weeks we would soon find out.

I had just dropped Jasmine off to daycare and was on my way back home when my phone rang with an unknown number. Hitting the hands free button on my steering wheel I answered as I made my way down the expressway.

"Hello?" I answered. It never bothered me picking up unknown calls since our credit was good and we paid all of our bills on time. But something about this one before I answered had me feeling uneasy.

"Chasiti?" the woman said. I hadn't heard her voice in almost three years and although I didn't hate her, I rather not talk to her.

"Chardonnay? Well how have you been?" I did my best to sound chipper and her not pick up on the hidden attitude I was trying my best to hide.

"I'm good. How are you feeling these days?" she asked me. For some reason she sounded unsure about this call and now my curiosity was piqued.

"Just fine thanks."

I had heard that a while after she had given her life to The Lord she moved away with her husband to another state. I didn't do too much gossiping so never did I ask where because I really didn't care one way or another.

I honestly had forgiven her and even made sure Gavon didn't throw his life away by killing her but I felt like my duty had been done and I could move on. This call was making me second guess the moving on part and I didn't know why.

“So what do I owe this pleasure of a phone call?” I asked hoping she would get to the point. By now I was hungry and a chicken, egg, and cheese biscuit from McDonald’s and a frozen lemonade from Chick-fil-a was calling my name something loud.

I giggled slightly thinking of how Mama Jean never called a chicken what it was but she always called it a yard bird. That old woman was a mess. Had she still been here she probably would have fussed out Chardonnay then hung up on her as soon as she heard her voice.

“Well I know that you’re almost ready to deliver but-“ she started before I cut her off.

"Wait. How do you know I'm about to have a baby?" Something wasn't right and I was about to catch a serious attitude.

"Um that's what I wanted to meet with you about. I've been seeing Gavon and I thought you should know." She said sounding uneasy.

Now I don't know what the enemy thought when he came up with this cockamamie attack but pregnant or not I was about to get to the bottom of this. What in the world did she mean by 'she has been seeing Gavon'?

All I could see was red as I pulled into the parking lot of Chick-fil-a and parked. I knew my pressure was up because these Braxton hicks were kicking in full force. If Chardonnay thought she was coming back into our lives to mess up what we had established then she had another thing coming. She wanted a fight? Then a fight she would get.

"Where are you?" I asked as I focused on getting my breathing under control.

"I was about to stop and get something to eat before heading to my realtor and get the keys for my new apartment, I just moved back to Savannah." She said. You could have knocked my big behind over with a feather at that bit of news.

"I'm at the Chick-fil-a on Pooler Parkway. Can you meet me here?" I asked her.

I needed God to intervene because I was getting myself worked up and didn't even know why. For all I know she could have been meeting him with her husband for counseling or something.

But if that was the case then why hadn't he let me know?

"Oh that's perfect. I was just about to stop and get me a frozen lemonade before I headed over to McDonald's. These pregnancy cravings are killer this go round."

"You're pregnant?" I asked.

I swear to God I'm going to jail at 37 weeks if the next words out of her mouth were the same ones I was thinking.

"Um. Gavon didn't tell you about me huh?" she said having the nerve to sound sad.

"No."

By now livid would be an understatement as I noticed a newer model Lincoln Navigator pull up to my right and park. Chardonnay looked into my eyes with hers filled with sadness and the phone still to her ear while she opened her driver's side door.

I couldn't lie she was looking flawless and I saw why Gavon used to mess with her back then. Besides being ratchet had she carried herself back then like she does now they may have worked one day. Just that thought alone made my stomach feel tighter but the sight before e made my chest tighten as well.

"We really need to talk then." She said still looking at me through the window as my eyes left her face and landed on her big round belly.

If that wasn't enough to send me under, the dampness I began to feel between my legs sure would. Fine time for my water to break huh?

COMING SOON

And just because I love my readers I'll just drop this right here.......

"What LIES Beneath: A Mother's Deception"

by Denora M. Boone

Chapter One

Monae

I looked around at the faces of the people surrounding the casket as it sat above the open hole in the ground. Some were crying tears and I was unsure if they were genuine or crocodile ones. I understood why I wasn't crying and that was because I felt nothing. No anger, no sadness, not even the confusion I felt for years was present as the pastor said a prayer and the workers began to lower down the dark oak box into its final resting place.

"Yall better watch out. The ground is going to burst open in flames as soon as she hit the bottom." I heard my brother Leviticus snicker.

The look I gave him shut him right on up because he knew that I was not about to play with him right now. I understood why he felt the way he did but this was not the time nor place to act out.

I watched as the medium height and built light skinned man moved closer to the hole holding a few roses. His words were inaudible like he was praying or maybe he didn't want anyone to hear what he was saying. I fought everything in me to not roll my eyes at this sight. He was definitely putting on a front and a big one at that.

"Does anyone have any last words they want to speak over the beloved?" the pastor asked.

It felt like time stood still and everyone was holding their breaths waiting to see if there would be one. I felt a hand resting on my lower back and I looked up into the face of my handsome husband. The wink he gave me let me know that he stood by me whether I decided to speak or not over the body that lay inside that coffin. Even at this very moment I was unsure of if I would or not. What would I say? What could I say? Do I tell the truth and have these people looking at me as ungrateful or do I lie and speak the blessed and highly favored words people wanted to believe? I wasn't taking that chance so I kept quiet.

The man who had just softly spoken over the body a few minutes before looked over at me and the people that stood beside me with an angry scowl on his face. I knew what he was thinking and he knew what we were thinking but I would never show out and air dirty laundry out at a funeral. This was not the place and that would be so tacky.

I turned my head back towards the front and noticed a tall dark skin man walking in our direction. At first I thought I was seeing things but soon my eyes revealed that he was indeed here. My father had always said that he would never want to see my mother again in life until she was dead and he would make sure that when she did die he would spit on her grave. That's exactly why I didn't tell him when I found out a week ago when she passed away. My father never lied to me a day in his life although some days I wish he had because he could just be too blunt at times, but I knew if he was here he was about to keep his word.

My stomach began doing flips and my heart felt like it was beating in my throat as time seemed to move at a snail's pace. I could hear my sisters began to breathe rapidly as my twin brothers began to snicker as we prepared to watch this madness unfold.

"Oh God no." I whispered.

"Is he about to do what I think he is?" My husband asked me.

Before I could respond my dad Joc hawked up as much spit as his mouth could hold and let it fly all over my mother's casket. I tried shielding my children from the sight before us but I couldn't take my own eyes off of it long enough to do so. My uncles were trying their best to take my father to *his* final resting place but none of them were a match for Jaquez "Joc" Hampton. He wasn't a big man but he was as strong as an ox and my uncles Tony and Jason were learning the hard way not to judge a book its cover.

I may not have been too fond of my mother but my daddy? That was my heart and if it wasn't for my children and my husband being there I would have probably been right beside him throwing bows.

Just as one of my uncles caught Joc off guard a shot rang out along with a clap of thunder that roared so loud it sounded like the sky was opening up and Jesus was soon to appear. I guess

God wasn't pleased at all because this right here was some straight shenanigans if I ever did see any.

"Now this here is enough! Y'all not gonna do this over my dead daughter's body! She was a good woman and I won't let her memory be tarnished. If you don't want to be here then leave!" my grandmother Markita said.

I would repent later because the look on my face displayed the bad taste she had so effortlessly put in my mouth. She had flat out lied calling my mother a good mother and if anything is tarnished it was because of the woman who was now just a shell of a being.

Without a single word I grabbed my husband's hand and let my children know it was time to go. My siblings all watched as I walked away from the site towards our car. I knew they would soon be behind me because our feelings over that woman that gave birth to us was surely the same.

"I don't know why you're even here Monae! Diamond never wanted you to begin with. Why do you think she never came looking for you when your grandparents took you? Since she found you again you have been nothing but a headache to her. I wish it was you in there and not my precious child because all of this is your fault." She nastily spoke as the real tears began falling down my face.

Before I knew it my hands were tight around my grandmother's throat and I felt people pulling on me trying their best to break us a part but I wouldn't let go. Too much anger that I had bottled up inside of me that I thought I had let go was now surfacing again. Since Diamond was no longer here to feel my wrath the one who gave birth to her sorry behind would do me just fine.

"Well she should have aborted me when she had the chance to." I firmly stated as I let her neck go and she fell to the ground.

I know that some of you are wondering why I'm so mad and hurt and ready to have my grandmother laying right beside her dear *precious* daughter. Well just sit tight and let me take it back to the beginning.

COMING SOON

I thank God for this journey that He has me on. To know that people are turning back to Him because of something He allowed me to write gives me so much joy!

Thank you to my loving husband and children for supporting me along the way. Not only do I sacrifice a lot but so do you all by understanding what is required of me and still loving me to the moon and back! I love you all!!

My AIP family is the best hands down!! Yall go just as hard for this company and I appreciate you all for what you do. No one is above anyone else and we all are family til the end. Jenica, Charles, Deedy, Tab, Kat, Latisha, Tammy,

Allison, and Andre thank you all for coming into my life!

My Kingdom Dominion Ministries family….the strength and love you have given to me and my family from day one is like nothing we have experienced before. No judgement or ridicule of who we were only love and acceptance of who God has called us to be. I love yall so much!

To all of my loyal readers and supporters I couldn't do it without you! Thank you for taking me with the highs and the lows and waiting patiently/impatiently for each of my releases! Lol!!

If you rocked with me from the beginning and suddenly stop then that love wasn't real from the gate but I appreciate that more than you will ever know! Was that a little petty? I'm sorry I'm working on my deliverance! Lmbo!!

#Love

Dee

Made in the USA
San Bernardino, CA
01 July 2016